ROAD TO
PERDITION™

ROAD TO
PERDITION™

A Novel by Max Allan Collins

Adapted from the Screenplay by David Self

Based on the graphic novel

written by Max Allan Collins

and illustrated by Richard Piers Rayner

AN ONYX BOOK

DREAMWORKS®

ONYX
Published by New American Library, a division of
Penguin Putnam Inc., 375 Hudson Street,
New York, New York 10014, U.S.A.
Penguin Books Ltd, 80 Strand,
London WC2R 0RL, England
Penguin Books Australia Ltd, Ringwood,
Victoria, Australia
Penguin Books Canada Ltd, 10 Alcorn Avenue,
Toronto, Ontario, Canada M4V 3B2
Penguin Books (N.Z.) Ltd, 182–190 Wairau Road,
Auckland 10, New Zealand

Penguin Books Ltd, Registered Offices:
Harmondsworth, Middlesex, England

First published by Onyx, an imprint of New American Library,
a division of Penguin Putnam Inc.

First Printing, June 2002
10 9 8 7 6 5 4 3 2 1

TM & © DreamWorks, 2002
Interior photographs by Francois Duhamel
Road to Perdition Key Art: Pulse Advertising/David Sameth
All rights reserved

For Richard and Dean Zanuck—
another father and son
who shared the road

"You must choose a road for yourself."

—Kazuo Koike

1

There are many stories about Michael Sullivan. Some say he was a decent man. Some say there was no good in him at all. But I once spent six weeks with him in the winter of 1931. This is our story.

He was brought to America when he was a baby, the family forever losing its "O" at Ellis Island, thanks to a careless slip of the pen. The newly (if accidentally) christened Sullivans soon settled in Rock Island, Illinois, where the promise of work at the John Deere and Harvester plants—and the government arsenal, where guns and tanks were manufactured—attracted many would-be laborers.

Immigrants in America, whether Irish or Italian or Jewish, quickly learned that local government ignored them; the only real government was what the Black Hand–type gangs provided. Little criminal kingdoms—subgovernments—grew up in cities all around America, thriving further with the onset of Prohibition. The Tri-Cities—Rock Island and Moline, on the Illinois banks of the Mississippi River; Davenport over on the Iowa side—

were no exception. And the ruler of the Tri-Cities was
John Rooney.

The Irish Rooneys had an unlikely but nonetheless
abiding affiliation with the powerful Italian/Sicilian
Capone gang in Chicago. John Rooney himself was a self-
trained lawyer, and considered by most Micks in the
Cities to be a benign presence, a benevolent despot. He and
his son, Connor—a glorified chauffeur for his father, and
widely considered a pale, rather unstable shadow of the old
man—had the politicians and police deep in their pockets.

In retrospect, it's hard to picture my father being any
part of such sleazy underhanded tactics. Michael Sullivan, Sr., was what they used to call a family man—quiet,
dependable, honorable; he didn't drink to excess, he didn't
whore around. And I know with soul-deep certainty that
he loved my mother . . . his Annie.

Yet there was indeed another, darker side to my father.
Though he never spoke of it to us, he was a proud veteran.
He had returned to Europe in 1916, to fight in the Great
War. He was decorated for bravery, having learned to use
a gun to kill other men, a sin in God's eyes that Uncle Sam
saw fit to reward him for.

So when Michael Sullivan came back from the Great
War he was good with a gun, and was hired by Mr. John
Rooney, serving him well, still a loyal soldier.

My father's alliance with Mr. Rooney went back to the
old country. Whatever bad things the Rooneys were involved in, the Micks of the Tri-Cities knew only that, despite hard times, old man Rooney got jobs for our people,
at his newspapers, his restaurants, the factories, and even

the government arsenal. Of course, to my father, and to many of his peers, John Rooney was the government.

I never knew exactly what Papa did for the Rooneys, just that he was good at his job. After all, we lived in the nicest house in town (except for Mr. Rooney's) and John Rooney treated my father like a second son, and my younger brother Peter and me like cherished grandkids. We loved Mr. Rooney—though we sensed our mother did not share that affection—and knew only that Papa did something dangerous for him . . . something involving a gun. Like Tom Mix, or the Lone Ranger.

Usually that gun was a Colt .45 automatic. We had seen him with that weapon, Peter and I, on many occasions—spying on him with pride and wonder as our father slipped the pistol into a leather holster under his coat, tucked under his shoulder. Once, however, we saw Papa with an even more formidable firearm, and the sight had fueled our whispered conversations deep into the night.

On that one occasion, we had spied him with his shiny black case: this hard-shell valise-type affair we had seen many times. But only once did our wide eyes observe its contents; only once did we (unseen by Papa) witness that case actually being opened.

The shiny black case might have protected a musical instrument—a horn, say, or a violin. However, the parts broken down within, in their plush little compartments, were those of a Thompson submachine gun. These pieces my father could assemble quickly, efficiently, into a single frightful unit. Last would come the drumlike canister of ammunition, which he snapped onto the assembled *weapon before closing the lid of the valise, flicking the latches until the shiny black case seemed harmless again.*

On his bike, pedaling furiously, Michael Sullivan, Jr.—hands warmly mittened, face obscured by a long woolen scarf, a satchel of newspapers slung over his shoulder—crested a hill and flew down a street whose gray cement was a solitary ribbon in a vast landscape of snowy white. Leaving the residential area behind, he was soon speeding along a vast stretch of closed factories—even Mr. Rooney's beneficence could not entirely wipe out this Depression—summoned by the whistle of one of the few remaining thriving industries.

Before long Michael—a slender pale kid with a thatch of brown hair, small for his age—was standing out in front of the gates of the John Deere plant, whose smokestacks billowed black as workers poured out to hear the paperboy's cry: "Man dies in factory accident! Man dies!"

The Deere factory was not one of the boy's usual corners to peddle his papers, but Mr. McGowan at Peerless Pharmacy—where Michael picked up his daily supply of the *Rock Island News*—had recommended that the boy go there. White-haired, bespectacled Mr. McGowan, the proprietor of the drugstore (though of course Mr. Rooney owned it), had said the workingmen at the plant would find this story of particular interest.

This bit of wisdom Mr. McGowan had served up

with the same twinkle in his eyes that might have accompanied an ice-cream soda.

And the toil-haggard men outside John Deere did
in fact reach into their pockets for nickels and dimes
to read the story of how Danny McGovern had
fallen into the machinery at Mr. Rooney's soft-drink
bottling plant.

UNAVOIDABLE ACCIDENT A TRAGEDY, a smaller head-
line said; and Michael had glimpsed in the write-up
how Mr. Rooney was generously bequeathing the
dead man's family a full two years' salary, though
"nothing but the goodness of John Rooney's heart
required it." The family couldn't afford a funeral
home, so Mr. Rooney was providing his own mansion for the wake.

But the twelve-year-old boy was wise enough in
the ways of the local press to know that the Rock Island *Argus*, Rooney's chief competition in the newspaper business, would present this story in an
entirely different light. The *Argus* called Mr. Rooney
"a gangster," among other equally unflattering
things, and the editorials in the two papers were like
the salvos of opposing battleships.

In under ten minutes, Michael had made a real
haul, and he was grinning—despite the bitter cold—
when he hopped back on his bike, pockets jingling
with change. He pulled on his mittens, threw the
scarf over his face, and streaked out of the industrial
area to the *klik-klik-klik* of the baseball card clothes-
pinned to his bike's back wheel, the card playing the
spokes like a brittle harp. He pedaled past the Har-

vester plant, gliding by one of the soup kitchens where Mr. Rooney saw to it that hungry out-of-work men at least got something warm to eat, then ducked down an alleyway between two huge warehouses, the chimneys of industry receding behind him.

Before long he was sailing past St. Peter's Church, its ominous Gothic spires looming behind the iron fence; then he cycled straight down the middle of Main Street's two lanes, drivers frowning and even cursing at him as, going in either direction, they narrowly missed the boy. Michael had played this dangerous game of auto tag for as long as he'd been hawking papers; he liked the exhilarating feeling it gave him.

Some of the stores were boarded-up, even on Main Street—often he had heard his father tell his mother, *We are lucky to have it so soft in such hard times*—but not the drugstore ... or any of Mr. Rooney's shops or restaurants, for that matter.

Michael parked his bike out front and sauntered in, dropping his newspaper bag on the counter. Mr. McGowan acknowledged the boy with a nod but immediately began counting out the few remaining papers. Unwrapping his scarf, Michael dug into his pocket for the change and deposited the coins on the counter, where they danced and rang. White face exposed, the boy drank in the scents of penny candy and pulp paper and tobacco—what a wonderful place a drugstore was.

The druggist quickly counted the coins, then glanced up, an unruly eyebrow raised, signaling to

Michael that the books were not balanced. And with a sigh, the boy again dug into his pocket, found the missing nickel, and slammed it onto the counter.

With a humorless smile, Mr. McGowan nodded, and returned to his calculating. While the druggist was counting out the meager coinage that would be the boy's commission, Michael surreptitiously sneaked a pouch of Bugler tobacco from the counter display and up under his coat, into the waistband of his trousers.

Pocket jingling with the nickels he'd earned (as opposed to pilfered), Michael strode out of the drugstore, onto the sidewalk, where he wheeled his bike around the corner into an alleyway.

Then, glancing around, he withdrew from a coat pocket a battered-looking brown briar pipe with a bit of a Sherlock Holmes shape to it, a smoking instrument that his father had thrown out a few weeks ago. Michael filled the bowl with tobacco, tamped it down, and fished a book of matches from another pocket, lighting up like an old pro.

Puffing the pipe as if that were powering him, Michael cycled out of the downtown area and into the nearby residential district, flush with that satisfying feeling known only by a kid who is putting one over on the grown-ups of the world.

When he finally coasted into the long, tree-lined driveway of the two-story structure that was the Sullivan home, Michael grew suddenly cautious. He should put the pipe away, he knew, before getting in range of the windows of the large house, set against an idyllic background of the snowy woods. If his father saw the boy puffing away, Papa would just kill him. . . .

As Michael slowed, contemplating that, an assassin took advantage of this momentary caution on the boy's part, and a projectile hurled with deadly precision knocked Michael off-balance—and off his bike, onto a pile of white, the glowing pipe flying, dying a sizzling death in a snowbank.

Stepping from behind a tree, in mittens and snowsuit, Peter Sullivan, age ten, also small for his age, laughed mercilessly, delighted that his snowball had done such a spectacular job of unseating his brother.

But Michael had survived many such onslaughts, and was already fashioning a snowball of his own, so deftly, so quickly, that Peter had no time to run: he was doomed to take Michael's shot in the forehead. The younger boy pitched into the snow and rolled to a stunned stop, staring upward, breath pluming.

Michael, too, was on his back, also "dead"—the smoke of his breath outdoing the dying embers of the pipe.

Neither boy noticed the woman in the kitchen window, their mother, Annie Sullivan, smiling. From this distance, she had not discerned the pipe—or else her smile might have curved into a scowl—and knew only that these daily attacks by the younger boy against his big brother represented affection.

Annie—approaching forty, a petite, quietly pretty, peaches-and-cream-complected woman in a quietly pretty blue housedress—was pleased that the two boys got along so famously. Often brothers could be rivals, even adversaries, and since her husband seemed to favor the youngest boy (who had almost died in childbirth), Michael might easily have resented Peter.

Right now the rumble of her husband's Ford sedan was making minor thunder, announcing the imminent arrival of the head of the house. What was Michael, Jr., doing out there? Making a snow angel?

In fact, the boy—still sprawled in mock death—was trying with his foot to bury the pipe in the snow, hiding it (he hoped) from his father, whose face turned rather blankly to the two boys as the big dark green Ford headed toward the freestanding garage at the end of the long driveway.

Peter, of course, chased after his father. Michael just watched. If he were to tag after his younger brother, all that would happen was that Papa would ruffle the younger boy's hair and smile at him while maybe, maybe if Michael was lucky, he'd get a nod. That he could live without.

In the kitchen, before the table had been set for supper, while their mother was still at the stove, Michael and Peter sat together and did their homework.

Michael envied his brother, who was something of a whiz at school; right now the kid was writing in his notebook like the pencil was doing its own thinking. Criminey, how did he do that? Michael, on the other hand, was slogging through his math problems as if he were trying to run in a snowdrift.

The older boy sensed his mother beside him—the fresh-scrubbed smell of her—and when he turned she was at his shoulder, smiling at him like the Madonna, whispering, "I'll help you with it later."

He grinned at her.

She kissed his cheek and said, "Go fetch your father."

Then she told Peter to clear the schoolbooks and help her set the table as her older boy padded off.

The house was pale plaster, greens and yellows against dark woodwork; his footsteps echoed off the hardwood floors. Not exactly a rich person's house, but Michael knew he lived better than any of his friends. He loved the smooth feel of the banister as he ran up the stairs, palm gliding over sculpted wood.

On the second floor, at the end of the hallway, the half-opened door of his parents' bedroom gave Michael a view of his father at the mirrored dresser. Even without Mama's summons, Papa was preparing for dinner—removing his cuff links and placing them in a small carved wooden box with other personal items; taking off his striped necktie and turning to lay it on the bed as if placing a baby in its cradle; finally slipping out of his jacket, revealing the dark leather holster and the weapon under his arm.

The boy didn't know it, but this was a Colt .45, Army issue, a weapon that his father—Michael Sullivan, Sr.—had brought home from the Great War.

Gun—holster and all—was soon on the bed as well, and it wasn't until Sullivan was removing his vest that he sensed his son, and slipped the vest on top of the weapon, concealing it.

Silence throbbed in the big house, the tick of the grandfather clock downstairs deafening; Michael felt like a bug out in the hallway, hoping his father wouldn't step on him and squash him.

"Pa. . . . Dinner's ready."

"Thank you."

The boy scrambled away, down the hallway.

And in the bedroom, Michael Sullivan, Sr.—a tall, muscular man, pale, blue-eyed, with dark hair and regular features touched by a pencil-line mustache— looked at his own reflection. The man in the mirror—or was it three men, in the three panes of glass?—seemed to know that the boy required attention.

At the kitchen table, in a scene typically formal for this little family, the boys sat silent and scrubbed, Papa in his white shirt, Mama in her blue dress.

Michael was wondering why his father hadn't said anything about the pipe yet; he hoped nothing would be said to his mother about it.

"Michael," Papa said.

Just the faintest edge in his father's voice.

Michael looked up sharply, and with his eyes begged his father for mercy.

"Will you say grace?"

Smiling, relieved, the boy bowed his head, folded his hands, and said, "Bless us, O Lord, for these Thy gifts which we are about to receive through the bounty of Jesus Christ, our Lord. Amen."

They all said, "Amen," and Mama began passing the food around. Through the meal Michael felt his father's eyes land on him occasionally, and he waited for the rebuke in front of his mother; but it never came. Another bounty from Jesus—or anyway from Papa.

And they began to eat.

Later, the boys were listening to the Lone Ranger on the radio in the parlor, and their parents were washing dishes in the kitchen—actually, Annie was washing, Sullivan drying.

"Ouch!" she said.

He asked her what was wrong.

"Cut myself." She'd been washing cutlery, a carving knife.

Sullivan ran cold water and put her finger under it. Then he examined the wound carefully.

"It's not deep," he said, fetching a scrap of cloth and wrapping it around her finger. He gazed into her china-blue eyes and kissed her hand in a courtly manner, a knight and his maiden.

"Better?"

She nodded, and smiled.

They returned to their dishes, while in the living room the parlor echoed with the radio's gunfire.

2

John Rooney's mansion was on Twentieth Street in the area known in those days as the Longview Loop—so-called because this bluff area had been made accessible first by horse-drawn trolleys and later electric streetcars. This was Rock Island's Knob Hill—full of doctors, lawyers, and old money.

My brother and I went to a private Catholic school—the Villa de Chantal—not far from the Rooney mansion. My legs start to ache when I think of pedaling my bike up that hill—and back then the streets were brick.

Wealthy though he was, Mr. Rooney was a man of the people—a Catholic. Most of Rock Island's wealthy Irish were Orangemen, while most Irish Catholics were laborers, skilled and unskilled. My father was working-class poor and had grown up in the area known as Greenbush. He'd been in a gang in that rough part of town, though thanks to Sacred Heart Church there had also been a baseball team and other more wholesome recreational activities.

Still, looking back, I can see that my father—when he

was my age—must have been a young roughneck. And when Mr. Rooney took my father under his wing, he gave our family a life my real grandparents could never have provided.

The next afternoon, a Saturday, the overcast sky suggested the imminent arrival of an overanxious night. Young Michael could think of better ways to spend any part of a Saturday than going to see a dead person; but he knew not to object—particularly since Papa had said nothing more about the infamous briar pipe . . . and had obviously not shared his son's dire misdeed with Mama.

Papa had gone out to pull the car around close to the house and get the engine going, to provide his family with a warm car on this cold day. And Michael was the first to join his father, scrambling into the backseat. Papa's eyes probed him in the rearview mirror.

"Michael," his father said.

"Sir?"

"It's a wake. I don't want to see those dice . . . okay?"

"No, sir."

He didn't care if the boy's godfather—Papa meant Mr. Rooney—instigated it: *no gambling.*

Michael asked his father how a wake was different from a funeral, and his father said it was a kind of . . . celebration. And the boy asked why anybody would celebrate someone dying.

Papa's eyes in the rearview mirror grew thoughtful, and then he explained that it was a celebration of the dead person's life—sort of a send-off.

Soon Papa was driving, Mama next to him, Michael and Peter in back, everyone in their church-going finery. The boys, like their father, wore suits with ties and vests. Papa was all in black, even his tie, and Mama's navy-blue dress was so dark it, too, was almost black.

"Papa?" Peter said.

"Yes," Papa said, his eyes on the road.

"Did you know him?"

Peter meant the man who died.

Papa said, "Not very well."

"How did he die?"

"He had an accident. At work."

This was no surprise to Michael; he knew this was the dead man in the headlines yesterday, whose family Mr. Rooney was helping out by holding the wake at his mansion.

"What happened?" Michael asked.

His father's eyes went from the road back to the rearview mirror. "He choked on his pipe."

Michael almost laughed—Peter, too—but then both stifled their mirth, as their mother glanced first at Papa, then at her eldest son, with her brow knit in curiosity. The boy felt lucky, at that moment, that his mother so seldom asked his father what he meant by the sometimes puzzling things he said.

For the first time, however, as their automobile rolled up the winding driveway, Michael viewed the Rooney mansion as not just impressive, but ominous. Probably the dark sky and the funereal occasion were giving him this impression, the boy knew . . . but the massive castlelike structure, with its sand-color brick and reddish tile roof and fat formidable twin towers bookending the main building, loomed like a haunted house. Maybe it was the vaguely Arabic archways mixed in with the otherwise medieval look of the place. Whatever the case, Michael shuddered, a chill running through him that had nothing to do with the winter weather.

Out in front of the mansion were a number of cars and, oddly, several trucks. Mourners of every social station—rich and poor alike bedecked in their finest apparel—were trouping up into the house with the weary inevitability of the occasion.

Mama was carrying a covered dish, the crock containing a stew that was something of a specialty of hers. The boys had taken the lead, heading up the cement steps to the landing where massive doors waited.

The boys stood on the stoop until their father opened the door for them; their mother, crock in hand, went in first, followed by Peter and Michael, then Papa, filing into a long, wide hallway that set the tone for the mansion. They had entered into a high-ceilinged world of walnut paneling and mahogany trim, of parquet floors and oriental rugs, Tiffany lamps and velvet upholstery, ornate mirrors and shimmering chandeliers.

Despite the Sunday finery, it was clear even to an eleven-year-old like Michael that many of the mourners in this entryway contrasted sharply with the lavish surroundings. These were grizzled workingmen and their careworn wives and their scruffy children, sometimes grandparents, too, ancient-looking with sunken eyes and wrinkled-paper skin and Sunday clothing that dated to the turn of the century.

Hat in hand, their father was guiding them through this chattering, sometimes laughing throng, toward a sitting room.

In that room, a respectful silence, even an anguished one, was indeed on hand, draping the proceedings like a shroud. Relatives and friends were gathered here, seated on all sides. A parlor to the left, its doors folded open wide, served as the visitation area. Elaborate flower arrangements surrounded the open coffin, which rested on a bed of ice, buckets catching dripping water.

Michael and his father were walking in lockstep toward the coffin, but his brother, Peter, and Mama lagged behind.

Wide-eyed, horrified, Peter came to a stop and tugged his mother's sleeve. She looked down at him as he looked up with eyes that said he did *not* want to go up there.

"It's all right, honey," she said gently. "Come on. . . ."

But Peter held his ground, and Mama gave in. They stood just inside the room as Michael and his father went to the coffin and knelt before it and prayed.

Michael was wondering what the ice was for when his father leaned over to him and said, "It helps preserve the body."

The boy was still praying when he peeked over the casket rim. The dead man looked strange: his skin was waxy, pale as spilt milk; his lips and cheeks touched with clownish red; and weirdest yet, pennies covered his eyes.

Later Michael would ask his father what that was about, and Papa would explain that this was the toll the man paid to get into heaven. When the boy asked Papa if that worked, Papa admitted he didn't know—but they would light a candle for the deceased at St. Pete's, just to make sure.

Sneaking a sideways glance, Michael saw his father was still praying—something intense in his face.

"Amen," Sullivan said finally.

They got to their feet, and turned away from the casket.

That was when a husky, unmistakable brogue-touched voice boomed through the room. "Who's got a hug for a lonely old man?"

The attention of all four Sullivans flew to the commanding presence standing just inside the room, in a dark, tailored suit, his arms thrust wide: John Rooney.

The two boys ran to their substitute grandfather, filling his outstretched arms.

Annie Sullivan watched, fighting feelings of contempt for the man who had done so much for them. The lanky, almost-tall, white-haired, white-mustached paterfamilias had been a rakishly handsome young man. And even now, in his seventies, his powder-blue eyes, prominent cheekbones, and strong chin gave him the sort of distinctive good looks many a lady (though not Annie) still sighed over.

But of late Annie noted a certain shambling gait, and a wearied, even haunted expression, that indicated John Rooney might feel some small burden from carrying so many sins on his shoulders. She sometimes felt a hypocrite, knowing she and her family thrived thanks to this devious devil; and she tried not to think of what deeds her husband might be carrying out for the godfather of their sons.

And the boys did so love this old man.

Rooney was playing a game with them that was almost a ritual by now. "Now which is which?" he said, gazing down at the boys, a pointing finger traveling from Michael to Peter and from Peter to Michael.

Peter began to identify himself.

"Don't help me"—a fingertip touched one nose—"Peter"—then another nose—"and . . . Michael."

The boys groaned and laughed at this purposeful misidentification.

An arm around each boy, Mr. Rooney looked across the room, where Papa and Mama stood side by side now, the casket just behind them.

"Annie," he said quietly, with a nod. "Mike . . . good to see you."

Michael twitched a small smile, shrugged a little.

Mr. Rooney bent his head. To Michael he whispered, "D'you bring the necessary?"

Michael nodded, but eager Peter said, "Yes!"

Mr. Rooney stood, still with his arms around his godsons, and said to Papa, "I have urgent business with these gentlemen. Please excuse us."

Sullivan watched as Rooney led the boys away, in a conspiratorial huddle, and knew exactly what they were up to, and could only smile about it. A little.

Moving into the sitting room, various mourners and Rooney minions nodding to him respectfully, Sullivan made his way to a table piled with food and drink—appetizers, sandwiches, punch, hard liquor. He helped himself to a glass of whiskey: he needed it.

When he raised the glass for a sip, Sullivan noticed brawny Fin McGovern, in his best suit, standing nearby—a bottle of bourbon held in one hand like a Molotov cocktail he was about to throw.

McGovern—in his forties, the oldest of the brothers who had just lost their youngest, Daniel, the man in the casket—seemed to be studying Sullivan. His eyes might have glared had they not been slightly bleary.

In the basement of the mansion, Sullivan's youngest son had removed a shoe, tilting it to allow a pair of dice to roll from the toe into the heel. The boy plucked out the dice and passed them to Mr.

Rooney, who said solemnly to his godsons, "Gentle-men—let's shoot craps."

Michael watched with delight as the old man shook the dice in his cupped hands, then shook them some more; the old man kissed his clasped hands, tossed the dice in the air, caught them deftly, before lifting his left leg and firing them at the far cement wall, from which the dice bounced and rolled to a stop to the tune of the boys' laughter.

Mr. Rooney had a grace to him, and a sense of fun, that gave Michael a warm glow.

A little later, Mr. Rooney sat on the floor, his back to the wall, apparently devastated, mopping his brow with a handkerchief. He'd been wiped out by the boys of an astonishing sum: one dollar.

"Call the cops!" the old man demanded.

Mr. Rooney had already reminded them that the Chief of Police was upstairs, and that there were laws against highway robbery.

"I know hustlers when I see 'em," their godfather growled.

"No hustle, ol'-timer!" Michael said gleefully.

"Pay the man!" Peter said, hands on his hips.

Mr. Rooney held out his hands and the boys each took one to help him up, but their godfather was the one hustling: he pulled them down to him, drawing them close, arms around them as he kissed their foreheads. The boys hugged the old man back.

"Michael," Mr. Rooney said. "Fetch your dollar—jacket pocket in my study—before I change my mind."

Michael ran up the steps and then wove through the throng of mourners and took the big winding stairway up to the second floor, where most of the lights were out. Though night had not yet fallen, the overcast day added to the general gloominess of the big house with its dark woodwork and Victorian furnishings, and the boy's giddy mood shifted straightaway into apprehension.

Mr. Rooney's study was at the end of the corridor—Michael had sat with his godfather in the book-lined room several times, and they'd even played craps up there before. So he knew his way and went in, but the darkness of the room and the smell of cigar smoke turned his uneasiness to fear.

On the leather couch to one side of the chamber, Connor Rooney had stretched out, in his vest and shirtsleeves, a glass of dark liquid balanced on his stomach; he was smoking a cigar and the scent of it hung in the air, rich, masculine, nasty. Lanky, hooded-eyed, Connor was in his thirties, a dark blond handsome fellow who resembled his late mother.

Connor looked right at Michael, his face blank in that way Papa sometimes had. "Hello."

". . . Hello."

Michael and his godfather's only son were alone, Connor's cigar glowing orange in the darkness.

"Remind me—which little Sullivan are you?"

"Michael, sir."

" 'Sir?' " Glass of dark liquid in hand now, Connor

leaned up on his elbow and his grin looked weird. "You don't have to call me 'sir.' I'm not your pa."

Michael, wondering what Connor was doing off alone with the house full of guests, said, "No, Mr. Rooney."

"Call me Connor. Uncle Connor. Huh? What do you want?"

"Mr. Rooney sent me to get his jacket."

"You come back later, huh? I'm busy."

"Yes . . . sir."

With a shrug, Connor looked away from the boy, stretching back out, resting the drink on his stomach again, puffing on the cigar and making smoke rings, whose floating ascent and ultimate demise he studied with those weird, half-shut eyes of his.

Michael looked at the jacket over the back of the chair, where the dollar his godfather owed him awaited; but it seemed miles away, and he was scared. Connor Rooney frightened him and he wanted to get out of there, right now.

So he did.

3

John Rooney's mansion provided an unrivaled view of the Mississippi River Valley, including the mansions below his own on the bluff, which of course allowed him to look down on high society. In those days, only one bridge joined the Illinois and Iowa sides of the river—the government bridge, giving access to Arsenal Island from both shores—and most folks invested a nickel and crossed the Mississippi by ferry. This ferry included (after sundown) gambling and music.

Michael Sullivan, Sr., sat along the wall in a corner of the grand parlor, in a comfortable arm chair, by a softly glowing lamp on an end table beside him.

Somebody tapped a glass with a spoon, silence settled in, and all eyes—including those of Sullivan and Connor, who had come back downstairs from the study—were on John Rooney, who stood in front of an impressive fireplace.

Rooney looked out on the crowd, his sky-blue eyes

moving from face to face, making each of them feel he spoke directly to them.

"I welcome you all to my home," he said.

Rooney's brogue seemed thicker when he spoke in public, Sullivan thought.

"It's good to have so many friends in this house again. Since Mary died, it's just been me and my boy, walking around these big empty rooms. . . . Ah . . . I had a speech, but . . . truth is, it would be dishonest of me to say that I knew Danny well. But lose one of us, it hurts us all."

Around the parlor, murmurs of approval.

"I'll tell you what I do remember—and, Fin, you'll remember this, too—when Danny was on the high school football team? State championship: six points behind, ten seconds left to play . . . Danny threw the block of his lifetime . . . and tackled his own quarterback!"

Gentle laughter rippled across the room.

"Mistakes—we all make 'em, God knows." Rooney gestured around the room. He stood tall; his voice turned somber. "We drink today in Danny's honor."

Around the room glasses and bottles appeared, held high in the fashion of a toast, saluting the dead man. Watching this carefully, Michael Sullivan—on his feet now, as was everyone in the room but the musicians behind their stands—casually removed a small silver flask from a jacket pocket. He was not aware that his wife Annie—standing between their two boys, a protective arm around either—watched him closely, studying him as he listened to his "father" speak.

His voice strong, loud, Rooney said, "Let us wake him to God." Then his voice grew even louder, and wry humor touched it now. "And may he be in heaven an hour before the devil finds out he's dead."

Standing in back with his mother, young Michael—who had never before heard this traditional Irish commemoration—found the words fascinating, and disturbing. Why would a good person need to fool the devil? Had the man with the pennies on his eyes been a sinner?

Mr. Rooney was now introducing the brother of the dead man.

Michael Sullivan, Sr., was observing this tableau carefully.

"And now our good and trusted friend, Fin McGovern, will say a few words"—Rooney somehow managed to be light and serious at the same time— "words I'll wager got a little more poetry than these. . . . Fin, get up here!"

The burly brother of the deceased came to the front of the room.

"Thank you, John." Then the roughneck in his Sunday best turned toward the assembled mourners with a written speech. "My brother, Danny, wasn't wise, nor was he gentle."

Smiles and nods blossomed around the room.

"And with a skinful of liquor in him," McGovern said with a smile, though the moisture in his eyes glistened enough for Sullivan to see, halfway back in the crowd, "he was a pain in the ass."

Now a gentle wave of laughter rolled across the assemblage. Sullivan, however, was not smiling. With a glance at John Rooney, Sullivan and Connor rose and moved subtly toward the front of the room in case Fin suddenly grew belligerent.

"But he was loyal," the burly brother was saying of his brother, "and brave. And he never told a lie."

An uncomfortable silence was settling over the crowd.

"He'd have enjoyed this party," McGovern continued, rocking a bit, his unsteadiness showing. "Me and the family, we want to say thank you to our generous host."

These words seemed to relieve the mourners, the sarcasm not registering on many of them—though Sullivan knew. As did Annie.

"Where would this town be without Mr. John Rooney, God love him," McGovern said, his voice trembling.

A murmur of approval and clapping undulated over the room, Rooney bowing his head, humble, grateful for such kind words.

On wavering feet, McGovern turned to Rooney, studying him. "I've worked for you many years now, John . . . nearly half my life. And we have never had a disagreement. . . ."

Few in the room could have noted the shift in John Rooney's expression—the steel coming into his eyes. Sullivan did. He was already slowly working his way forward in the crowd, Connor following close behind.

"But I have come to realize," McGovern said, voice quavering, "that you rule this town as God rules the earth. . . . You give and you take away."

And Sullivan was onstage now, making sure his expression seemed friendly as he took Fin McGovern's arm—gentle but firm in his grasp—and walked him off the stage, as the mourners watched, uneasy, not certain what they had just witnessed.

"Strike up the band!" Rooney commanded buoyantly, and the musicians began a bouncy reel, as the host turned to the assembled guests with a smile and another raise of his bottle. Sullivan had already hustled the grieving, drunken brother out the front door, two of McGovern's friends emerging from the crowd to follow.

At the back of the room, protective arms again around the shoulders of her boys, Annie watched—trying not to let alarm show in her face—as Connor Rooney stepped from the sidelines to follow after her husband and Fin McGovern . . . and two of Fin's tough roughneck chums.

The three of them headed for the buffet table, though Annie glanced back several times, not showing her worry, though her older boy sensed it, anyway. As his mother helped Peter maneuver a piece of cake onto a small plate, Michael slipped away.

The boy walked out the front door, which was ajar. He saw Mr. Rooney, his back to Michael, standing in darkness, looking out on the driveway and front lawn, at a small commotion.

Michael's father was guiding the deceased's brother, Fin McGovern, walking the big man toward a truck, where two more big men had gone on ahead, waiting, their nasty expressions at odds with their funereal fineries. Connor Rooney was bringing up the rear, trotting alongside Fin McGovern, who was almost falling down, he was so drunk.

Michael could recognize Fin McGovern's condition as drunkenness; and he even understood that the man had gotten this way out of his sorrow.

What surprised Michael was the vehemence, the savagery with which Fin McGovern refused Connor Rooney's help, shoving the man away, yelling, "I'm going to bury my brother. . . . Then I'm going to deal with you."

But Pa, on the other side of the drunken man, didn't seem to take this very seriously, just saying, "Sure, Fin, sure . . . you'll take care of us . . . after a good night's sleep."

Papa kept walking Fin McGovern toward that truck, where the two other big men were milling and grousing among themselves as they waited. As Papa helped Mr. McGovern up into the vehicle, the other men quieted down and lent a hand, then got in themselves, one behind the wheel, steadying Fin between them.

But Connor Rooney—once he'd been shoved—had stayed behind; and when he turned away from them, his face looked white and strange in the moonlight. Michael saw no expression in Connor's face, and yet he knew that the man was furious. What Papa had taken as a drunken remark, "Uncle" Connor seemed to consider a direct threat.

As the truck rumbled off down the driveway, its headlights cutting through the night like swords, Mr. Rooney stepped out of the darkness and went down the steps to join his son and Sullivan, who were heading back to the mansion. They met at the bottom of the porch steps.

"Is he all right?" Mr. Rooney asked, meaning Fin.

Shrugging, Connor said, "Yeah, he's fine. Just too much to drink. I'll talk to him."

But Michael knew Connor's casual words didn't match up with that awful expression the man had worn just moments before.

Mr. Rooney said, "All right. But take Mike with you."

"No, Pa—I'll be fine . . ."

"Take him with you," Mr. Rooney said sternly, as if Connor were a child, not a man. "And *talk* to Fin. Nothing more. . . . We've had enough rough stuff, for a while."

Michael glanced back to see if his mother had noticed his absence, and when he returned to his spying, Mr. Rooney was coming through the door!

But all his godfather did was tousle Michael's hair and smile down at him, before moving back into where the mourners were having their party. Connor ignored Michael, but Papa seemed surprised, and not happy, about seeing him.

And Michael Sullivan, Sr., wondered what his son might have seen and heard—and what the boy had understood.

While young Michael did not really comprehend why these supposedly sad people were having a party, he did enjoy himself as the festivities got more lively. Plenty more people were at least as tipsy as Mr. McGovern had been, dancing to the band, which played lots of different kinds of music.

The mourners seemed to like the reels best of all, and Mr. Rooney, charming host that he was, would shuffle across the room, nodding to people, sometimes chatting with them, a glass of whiskey in hand—sometimes two glasses.

Their mother danced with one of Mr. Rooney's men—she whirled around, her hair flying, looking as pretty as the young unmarried girls.

Connor Rooney turned out to be a really good dancer. Much as he didn't care for his so-called uncle, the boy enjoyed watching the man dance—he was really good, slick and smooth, like one of those dark handsome dancers in tuxedos in the picture shows.

Everybody kept an eye on Connor, and he got a lot of applause. Probably Connor's biggest fan was Mr. Rooney, and Michael could tell Uncle Connor liked that—maybe it made up for being treated like a kid, outside. When Connor finished up the latest reel, he executed a deft dip that didn't hide how drunk he was, or how pleased he was that Mr. Rooney was laughing and clapping and proud.

A gentle rainfall of piano notes—the opening chords of a melancholy tune—soon filled the room.

As "aaahs" issued forth from the crowd, all eyes were turning toward the piano, where John Rooney sat, playing. The room had gone otherwise silent when Rooney looked up, caught Sullivan's eye, and with a bob of the head, motioned him over. Moments later, Sullivan was sliding in next to the old man on the piano bench.

Annie, cup of coffee in hand, swiveled to watch. So did Michael, off to one side, eating a slice of cake. Peter somehow wound up standing next to Connor Rooney, and the two drank in the sight of their respective fathers melding musically, as Sullivan played along with Rooney, hesitant at first, but gradually catching up.

The beautiful melody caught people off guard, and the song soon had people swaying, eyes tearing. Something moved Michael, seeing his papa next to Mr. Rooney, who was so much like a father to Papa, just as he was like a grandfather to Michael and Peter. To see Papa playing so freely, beside Mr. Rooney, made the boy happy.

Annie Sullivan could only smile and shake her head a bit, knowing that her husband would do anything that terrible wonderful old man might ask.

Michael noticed his brother standing next to the scary Connor, who was also watching and smiling. The man's mouth was smiling, but his eyes sure weren't.

After the piano duet trailed off, Rooney turned to

Sullivan, put his arm around his shoulder, and the two men embraced.

Peter, next to Connor Rooney, looked at the grown-up next to him; the slender, slick-haired man was an odd duck, the boy thought—something really strange about his eyes.

But most of all, the really weird thing was how the man smiled all the time. Peter wondered about that, and being a child, he decided to ask.

"Why are you always smiling?"

And Connor Rooney looked down at him, the smile still going. "'Cause it's all so fuckin' hysterical."

The boy stood frozen for a few moments, then scurried off, disturbed, terrified, and yet strangely exhilarated at hearing the legendary swear word—the only other time he'd heard it, a schoolyard bully had been expelled for saying it.

But a grown man like Mr. Rooney's son couldn't be a bully—could he?

Several hours later, at home in his pajamas, Michael was in the hallway padding back from the bathroom when he heard muffled voices. Pausing by his parents' bedroom door, he could make out both his mother and his father talking . . .

Desperate to hear them, and yet not wanting to eavesdrop, he headed quickly back to the bedroom he shared with Peter. The lights had been officially out for some time, and Peter had been asleep for maybe half an hour; but Michael—as was his habit—was up late, reading.

Crawling back under the covers, he picked up the flashlight and held it over the book he was reading—*The Lone Ranger Rides*, a Big Little Book. He loved the fat little books, which were about four inches wide and four inches tall and two or three inches thick—on each page at left was text, and at right a full-page picture.

Most of the Big Little Books (ten cents each at the dimestore) featured comic strip characters like Dick Tracy and Little Orphan Annie; Michael's favorites, though, were the Western heroes, like Tom Mix from the movies and the Lone Ranger from radio. He flew through the thick books, gulping down the words, inhaling the pictures, each of which had a caption: "Moonlight streamed into the room." Unless he was in the middle of a sentence, he would always look at the picture first, and then read the caption, and finally the page of text. He flipped a page, revealing a shadowy figure climbing in a window: "A man climbed in the window."

The captions always told you what your eyes had already seen, yet somehow the repetition made everything seem more important, more suspenseful. . . .

"Michael?"

He jumped, even though it was just Peter's voice. "What?"

"I had a nightmare. . . . It was about Mr. Rooney's house."

"Peter, it's just a house. A big house. Go back to sleep."

Silence.

Then Peter asked, "Is Mr. Rooney rich like Babe Ruth?"

"Richer." Michael leaned on his elbow, thinking about his little brother's question. "Well, he's richer than the Babe . . . and the Babe is richer than the President."

"Are we rich?"

"No, stupid."

Michael heard Peter getting settled in his bed, again; relieved, the older boy returned to his reading. The first part of the story was about the bad things the outlaws did; later would be the good part, when the Lone Ranger got even.

"Michael?"

"What?"

"What's Papa's job?"

Looking at the Lone Ranger's picture—he was on his horse, next to Tonto, his Indian friend—Michael said, "He works for Mr. Rooney."

"Why?"

"Well, Papa didn't have a father. So Mr. Rooney looked after him."

"I know all that. But what's his *job*?"

Michael turned the page. The picture was of Beasley, the rancher, in his bed at night, sitting up to turn toward the sound *klik!* And the caption read, "Beasley heard the click of a gun."

Michael said nothing, studying the picture of the frightened rancher.

Finally Michael said, "He goes on missions for Mr. Rooney. . . . They're very dangerous—that's why he takes his gun. . . ." Michael turned the page. "Sometimes even the President sends Papa on missions—because Papa was a hero in the war and all."

Peter, sitting up now, covers in his lap, thought that over. Finally the younger boy said, "You're just making that up."

"I am not!"

Peter rolled over in bed, with a sigh, facing the wall as he said, "It's all so fuckin' hysterical. . . ."

Alarmed, Michael sat up. "Peter—Peter, don't ever say that word."

"Okay." Peter curled back up in bed, chastised.

Michael put the Big Little Book, folded open to his place, on his nightstand. The boys said good night to each other, and Michael hoped he wouldn't have any nightmares. If he did, he figured it wouldn't be that house or even the dead body that gave them to him, or even the Frankenstein monster.

Most likely it would be the boogeyman that was Uncle Connor.

4

My brother Peter and I attended a private Catholic school, a sprawling Gothic affair with spires and stained glass peeking through trees on the bluff—not far from the Rooney mansion, actually.

I remember some of the other kids whispered about Peter and me at school, because our father worked for John Rooney. I remember my confusion that the gentle man who was my godfather was also the stuff of grisly legend. Most kids would never cross Twentieth Street, not wanting to go near the looming Rooney house. You see, older children told the younger ones that Rooney was hiding in his mansion, waiting to capture little children and take them inside and grind them up into sausages.

Peter and I used to laugh about that, but sometimes the laughter would catch in our throats. Even then I think I knew that we had led a sheltered existence, and the inklings that our life was somehow a lie had begun to take shape in my youthful consciousness.

*   *   *

On the Monday morning after the Danny McGovern wake, the Sullivan family sat in their kitchen, having breakfast—or at least, the men in the family sat: Annie Sullivan was at the counter, preparing sack lunches for the boys. Sun, made brighter reflecting off snow, lanced through the windows, dust motes floating like pixie dust.

Peter was chomping at his last piece of crisp bacon, and Michael was slathering honey from a honeycomb on a piece of almost-burnt toast (the way he liked it), when their father put down his empty coffee cup, saying, "Peter, I'm sorry."

The younger boy looked up.

"I can't come to your concert tonight," Papa explained. "I'm working."

A meaningful glance flicked between the brothers, and Peter asked innocently, "Working at what?"

From behind them, at the counter where she was wrapping sandwiches in wax paper, their mother snapped, "Putting food on your plate, young man."

She always sounded more Irish when she scolded.

"All right, boys, clear your plates," Pa said.

Peter got up, placed his plate on the counter near the sink, then headed over to where his father sat. Sullivan opened his arms and embraced his younger son, saying, "You're a good lad."

Michael's feelings weren't hurt. He knew younger brothers always got more attention—they were the babies. But when the boy returned to the honeycomb for more sweetness, he made a nasty little discovery in one of the tiny holes: a dead bee.

Michael sat there frozen, hypnotized by the dead insect. Something about it . . . something about it . . .

"Michael?" his mother prompted.

"Huh?"

"Your plate."

"Sorry."

And he got up and cleared his plate into the trash—and threw his toast away, too.

At school, in history class, Michael sat at his desk toward the back, gazing out the window at the gray trees clumped with snow, a few brown leaves clinging desperately to skeletal branches. He was thinking about the dead man with the pennies on his eyes, and the dead bee, and the dead leaves . . . and it seemed to him suddenly that death was everywhere.

After school, after his paper route, Michael glided into the driveway on his bike, surprised not to be greeted by his brother's usual snowball assault; he looked at the garage and thought about his father and how Papa'd said he had to work tonight. Would he take his gun? Was this another mission? The boy went into the house.

Night had fallen—and a light rain had begun to fall as well—by the time Sullivan left the dry warmth of his home for the wet chill outside. The Clemens family—who had a girl Peter's age, also in the choir—had already picked up Annie and Peter to take them to the Villa for the concert. Michael was staying behind, up in his room, getting ready for some test or other.

In his dark topcoat and fedora, Sullivan strode through the drizzle to the garage, stepped inside, and moved to the rear of the building, to the cupboard, which he kept locked. Using a small key on his chain, he opened the doors and revealed boxes of ammunition, several handguns, and a black hardshell case that might have, but did not, house a musical instrument. With the weapon within the case in mind, he also selected, from the back on the upper shelf, two circular magazines—each drum containing one hundred .45-caliber cartridges, the same as he used in his handgun of choice, the Colt he'd brought back from the Great War.

Carrying case in hand, cartridge drums stuffed under an arm, Sullivan shut the cupboard up, relocked it, and walked to the garage doors, which he swung open; he got into the front seat, behind the wheel, reaching back to place the black case on the floor next to the rear seat, setting the drum-style magazines atop it. Then he started the vehicle up and the green Ford sedan rolled out into the light rain. He paused only to get out and close the garage doors again, unaware that—in the back of the car, inside the compartment under the rear seat—his son Michael, Jr., had stowed himself away.

The rain began to gather intensity, at first tap-dancing on the roof of the Ford, then drumming on it. Sullivan drove slowly—the streets were wet and slick, their surface a black mirror throwing street-lamp glow and the headlights of other cars back at him. Still, it took less than ten minutes to guide the Ford from the Sullivans' residential neighborhood to the downtown of Rock Island.

When Sullivan pulled up in front of the Florence Hotel, Connor Rooney was waiting, watching, just inside the lobby doors. The lanky Connor—in a black raincoat, his fedora snug—ran to the car, as if he could beat the rain there, and practically threw himself into the front seat.

They were less than five minutes from the warehouse district, even in this weather.

The sleepy-eyed Connor plucked a flask from inside his dark topcoat. "Want a shot?"

Sullivan shook his head. The last thing Connor needed was a shot—Sullivan could tell this one wasn't the man's first of the night.

Sullivan threw him a hard look. "We're just talking—all right?"

The only sounds were the wheels on wet pavement, the patter of raindrops on the roof, and the sloshing of gathered water in gutters.

"Let's not drag this out all night—I got to get myself downtown," Connor said casually.

At least the volatile younger Rooney appeared to be in an even temper.

As the Ford jostled over the slick streets, the lid of the rear seat lifted slightly, and the boy hidden away in the compartment got an inadvertent glimpse of the hard black carrying case resting on the floor, stuffed between the seats. The boy had only seen the inside of that case once, when—spying with Peter on their father—he'd watched Papa open it and assemble the parts within into a fearsome weapon.

He knew it was what the G-men on the radio and at the movies and in the funnies called a "tommy" gun—why its name was Tommy, the boy had no idea. Stuffy inside the cubbyhole, he pushed the lid up just enough to let in some air—but also to have another look at that hard-shell case before him . . . knowing what lay within.

Up in the front seat, Papa was driving and Uncle Connor was riding—Michael had recognized the unpleasant man's voice all too readily. They weren't talking anymore, though Uncle Connor was singing a jazz song; he seemed in a good mood.

Sitting on top of the hard-shell case were two round metal canisters—each about the size of a can of tuna fish, maybe a little bigger, bouncing a little as the car rolled over the pavement and its occasional potholes. The canister had something to do with the tommy gun—that time he and Peter had seen Papa assembling the weapon, the drum had been the last puzzle piece to get locked in place.

Michael was pretty sure the canister had something to do with bullets. He lifted the seat lid a few more inches; the canisters, jostling gently with the rhythm of the car, were easily within his reach . . . he could take one and look at it for a second and put it back, no one the wiser. . . .

That was when his father rounded a corner a shade sharply, and one of the canisters slipped off the black case, hitting the floor with a metallic *klunk*. With one hand on the wheel, and both eyes on his driving, Papa reached his other hand back, and Michael let the lid softly shut, not seeing his father fishing for the case, finding it, steadying it.

Again the boy lifted the lid slightly, peeked out, and saw the tommy gun canister balancing on end, like a little wheel, on the floor next to the case. His father's hand found the other canister, atop the case, and was now feeling around for the other one.

Michael reached for the canister, to put it back where his father would expect to find it, only the drum began to roll with every bump of the road. Finally, as his father took another corner, the canister glided into Michael's grasp!

The thing was heavy, much heavier than Michael had ever imagined, but he managed to put it back on top of the hard-shell case.

But as he drew his hand away, ready to slip back down into the darkness of his hideaway, Michael noticed a slot in the circular can: a bullet was showing!

He'd been right—it *was* bullets, bullets for the tommy gun . . . and reaching out tentatively with a forefinger, like every child who ever touched a hot stove, the boy put his fingertip against the cold metal of the bullet . . .

. . . and the bullet popped out!

He caught it, watching as another jumped into the slot. With his shoulder, he kept the lid up an inch or so, to let in enough light to see his prize. The bullet in his palm was two shades of metal; the Lone Ranger used silver bullets, but this one was made of something else.

Its lights doused, the Ford pulled down a narrow alley between brick buildings in an industrial area, though the boy—tucked away in his dark box under the backseat, his father's bullet tight and cold in his clenched hand—didn't know that. All he knew were sounds, like the hammering of rain on the Ford's metal roof, and the slice of sight he gave himself by lifting that lid a crack.

Then the car rolled to a stop, and Michael heard first Connor's door opening and closing, then his papa's, footsteps slapping at water-pooled pavement. And the back door opened, his father leaning in.

Michael eased the lid shut, returned to the womb of darkness, shivering, not just with the cold of the night.

The boy could hear that hard-shell case snapping open, followed by mechanical clicks and scrapes and clacks of machine-made parts fastening into other metal parts. That last metallic crack, Michael just knew, was that canister of bullets snapping on, like a terrible, wonderful period on the end of a sentence.

That was followed by another sharp closure—the back door shutting—making Michael flinch in his cubbyhole. The boy knew he shouldn't be here—even sensed, to some small degree at least, the foolhardy dangerousness of his own mission. But he was nonetheless as thrilled as he was frightened. What brave thing was his father doing on this dark rainy night? What injustice was he righting?

Michael waited forever—perhaps as long as a minute—and pushed up the seat lid and pulled himself out from the seat, staying low. The sound of raindrops pelting the Ford was louder out here, like God had His own tommy gun. Peeking over the front seats, the boy looked out the rain-streaked windshield into the night.

Blurry as his view was, Michael could tell he was in an alley, a wall of brick on either side. But where were his father and Uncle Connor?

There they were! Down standing under a yellowish lamp over a back entrance to the building. Was it a warehouse? Uncle Connor was knocking on the door; Papa was standing just behind him with something at his side—*the tommy gun?* To get a better look, Michael crawled carefully up and over into the front seat, trying not to make noise, though the pounding rain would have covered most anything. He got too close to the windshield, though, his breath fogging it, and when he wiped his own haze away with a jacket cuff, Papa and Uncle Connor were gone, the yellow lamp glowing alone in the night, like a drenched firefly.

He had come to watch his father "work"—to observe the dangerous, unfathomable things Papa, the war hero, did for Mr. Rooney. And inside the brick building, Papa was on one of those missions Michael and Peter had speculated about deep into so many nights, sometimes till after ten.

So, decision made, jaw firmly set—he was his father's son, after all—the boy stepped out into the downpour and sought to do what he'd done so often: spy on his mysterious old man.

He tiptoed through the puddles, making little splashes, hugging the nearer brick wall, staying in the shadows in case Papa and Uncle Connor came back out unexpectedly. He wasn't afraid of being left behind—the boy knew Rock Island well, from his paper route, and he could find his way home, though in this rain he might catch his death. But a cold was a risk worth taking. . . .

At the door, he could hear voices within, muffled, faint. No good. He needed to *see* inside, so he looked around for a window to peek in, or . . . *ah!* Just down the alley a ways was another door, a smaller one, the bottom of it not snug, the wood rotted away, allowing light to spill out into the wet alley like glowing, glistening liquid.

He knelt there, as if at an altar, and peered under the generous gap, which gave him a view inside of a huge, gloomy warehouse. It was a mostly empty expanse but for stacked crates and boxes and two men, out in the middle of the big room with its brick walls and concrete floor.

Fin McGovern was sitting in a chair, in a brown topcoat and no hat, hands in his lap; the other was Uncle Connor, in his drenched raincoat, standing in front of the seated fellow, walking back and forth a little, getting water on the floor, talking while Fin McGovern just listened, though he was looking at the floor, not at Connor.

Michael could not see his father, unaware that Sullivan was standing to one side of the door under which the boy peeked. And of course Sullivan—cradling his Thompson submachine gun in his arms like a baby—knew nothing of the boy's presence, though he had noted the figures back in the darkness of the warehouse, undoubtedly two of McGovern's cronies, who would be well armed themselves.

Both father and son, from their similar vantage points, listened and watched while Connor Rooney talked to Fin McGovern, their voices loud and hollow and ringing in the big room.

"Don't get me wrong, Fin," Connor was saying. "I feel for ya. I do. But you can't let a thing like that give you cause to go mouthing off."

McGovern said nothing, just sat in his chair and stared at the floor.

Connor leaned in from one side of the seated man. "You and my dad go back many years. He's a just man. So what do you say?"

McGovern shifted in his chair and sat there, silent.

"Come on now, Fin, let's make this easy," Sullivan said, stepping in front of the door.

The boy—hearing his father's voice just beyond that door, his view now partially obscured by Papa's feet—knew he should flee. But he couldn't help himself; he was fascinated by the tense tableau before him.

McGovern nodded, and perhaps spoke, but the boy couldn't hear him; the rain drowned out what might have been a whisper.

Apparently Connor had the same problem, because he said, "I can't hear you!"

"All right," McGovern said tightly.

Connor sighed and smiled. "Good. Thank you for such a civil meeting, Fin. And I am sorry. I'm sorry for your loss . . . I'm sorry for this misunderstanding . . . and I'm sorry your brother was such a fucking liar."

And with a self-satisfied smile, Connor headed away from the seated man, moving toward the door where Sullivan waited.

Sullivan—troubled by that last unnecessary twist of the knife—knew trouble could well follow, and his hands tightened around the machine gun.

And indeed (though the spying boy couldn't see them, from his gap-at-the-bottom-of-the-door vantage point) those two men of McGovern's—looking like the workers they were in caps and woolen jackets—stepped from the shadows with their rifles in their hands.

McGovern sat silently. Sullivan could tell that the man had been wrestling with himself, going along with these indignities for the good of the cause; but Connor had gone too far.

"My brother was not a liar," McGovern finally said, loud and unafraid.

Connor stopped and glanced at Sullivan with a slight smile. The man was enjoying himself, Sullivan knew, and it sickened him.

Turning to McGovern, apparently unimpressed by the two armed men, Connor said coolly, "Excuse me?"

McGovern spoke again, chin high. "To protect my family, and keep my job, I'll stay quiet. But don't think I don't know something's going on. And don't think I won't find out."

Connor seemed tense now, his voice threatening. "What are you saying, Fin?"

The men behind McGovern hoisted their rifles.

And McGovern raised a hand, first to Sullivan, then to his own men, saying, "Easy. We're just talking."

Connor nodded as if he agreed with that assessment.

"You tell your father, my brother never stole from him. I've checked the books—he never sold no booze to no one. Every single barrel is accounted for . . . and anyway, if he'd'a sold it, where's the money?"

Suddenly defensiveness colored Connor's voice. "How the fuck should I know? D'you check his *mattress*?"

"Maybe," McGovern said with a nasty smile, "you should check yours."

Hands stuffed in his topcoat pockets, Connor began to pace; his voice took on an edge that reminded Sullivan why the man had been nicknamed "Crazy Connor" since his childhood.

"You know, there's something immoral here," he was saying, and he turned toward Sullivan. "Don't you think so, Mike?" Then to McGovern, Connor said, "My beloved father, sentimental fool that he is, throws your little brother, your undeserving little brother, the wake of his life, and *this* is your thank you? What a hideous world this is."

Sullivan's spirits had fallen, even as his hackles rose: had he been in charge of this "talk," both sides would have shaken hands and gone about their business. Now violence was in the air. . . .

McGovern spoke harshly. "You think you're *smart*? You think I don't *know*? You've been spending so much time in Chicago, it's—"

Connor's hand flew from his pocket and the pistol in his fist bucked once, putting a bullet into McGovern's head. Stunned, surprised at his own death but without time to come to terms with it, the big man flopped sideways onto the cement floor.

That was still happening when the two men behind McGovern raised their rifles and Michael Sullivan opened fire with the Thompson, round after round chewing the men up and spitting them out, shaking them like naughty children, dropping them to the floor like the meat they'd become, unfired rifles clanking impotently on the cement, streaming blood seeking drains.

It happened so fast Michael wasn't sure what he was seeing, such a blur of activity the boy didn't even rear away, such a thunder of gunfire his ears seemed to explode, as he froze in wide-eyed horror and fascination, viewing the scene of carnage between his father's feet, shell casings falling and tinkling like wind chimes.

One of the men had fallen directly in Michael's view, a bloodied face with unseeing eyes, and the boy tried to move, tried to run, but he couldn't. His body seemed stalled, as if its engine wouldn't start.

And then he began to cry. He had seen death, and it hadn't been like Tom Mix at all, and his father was no Lone Ranger; the Lone Ranger shot guns out of bad men's hands—his father had gone another way altogether. Michael lay in a fetal ball and wept and the sky joined in, crying down on him.

Within the warehouse, Sullivan was furious. "What the fuck was that?"

Connor, as exhilarated as he was frightened, was breathing hard. "We're outta here."

"Jesus, Connor! *That's* your idea of 'talk'? What were you thinking?"

But John Rooney's son was moving quickly toward the door, leaving the scattered trio of bleeding corpses behind like so much refuse.

"Hey!" Sullivan said. "Don't walk away from me. . . ."

Suddenly, Connor stopped, but not at Sullivan's bidding.

Connor looked sharply at Sullivan. He pointed— a small hand was visible just under the ragged, rotted-away lower edge of the door.

Michael Sullivan, Sr., knew. He didn't know how he knew, but he knew: that small white hand belonged to his son Michael, Jr.

And he ran to the doorway.

The hand disappeared, and Sullivan pushed open the door, barging into the alleyway, where Michael stood in the darkness and the rain, slump-shouldered. Seeing his father with the tommy gun at his side, its snout still curling smoke, the boy recoiled, but he did not run.

"Oh Jesus, Michael. . . ."

Once his father had seen him, that was that, and he just stood there, letting the rain and his father have him. Stern as he could be, Papa was a kind father—he had never hit either of the boys. Though he had seen his father killing people, Michael felt not afraid, but rather ashamed for what *he'd* done, for the line *he'd* crossed. . . .

His father approached, slowly, quietly. "Michael, are you hurt?"

Michael said nothing at first, then shook his head. Uncle Connor filled the doorway—the man had that same terrible expression as in the moonlight; the door framed him, making an awful portrait.

Thompson still clutched in one hand, Sullivan knelt before his son, rain streaming down the boy's face like a thousand tears. "You saw everything?"

The boy nodded.

Saying, "Oh, Jesus," under his breath, Sullivan glanced back at Connor, who was approaching from the doorway, slowly. His mind reeled as he calculated a new host of dangers; then he looked at his boy, shivering in the rain.

"You must never speak of this to anyone. Do you understand? Not to anyone!"

The boy was shivering—was that a nod?

Connor ambled up beside Sullivan, who stood again. "Is this one of yours?"

To the boy these were two nightmarish figures before him, not his father and "uncle." They were both looking at him strangely, like the boy was a puzzle they couldn't figure out.

"Must've been hiding in the car," Sullivan said.

Finally, Connor let out a smile, but it was a ghastly thing. "Can he keep a secret?"

"He's my son."

Never had three words carried more weight.

The two men looked at each other, the rain pummeling them, the brim of Connor's hat collecting water, his father's fedora funneling the moisture over the rim. Even the boy, shaken as he was, could sense the tension.

Then Connor lifted his shoulders in a shrug. "Good enough for me." He nodded toward the Ford, blocking one end of the alley.   "You take him home. . . . I think I'll walk." He turned his collar up. "Perfect night for a stroll."

And Connor Rooney walked the other way, footsteps splashing as he headed out into the pouring rain and a dark night, leaving behind three corpses, one father, and one son.

5

Before that dreadful night, I hadn't known who or what my father was. All I'd had to guide me were my childish enthusiasm, an imagination fueled by radio, comics, and the movies, and the natural hero worship my brother and I shared for Papa.

I never heard my father referred to as the "Angel of Death," and whether that phrase was ever actually applied to him—or was merely some journalist's contrivance—I can only guess. I suspect there's at least a grain of truth in it, because I did on occasion hear him called "Angel," by men we met on the road. But I'll never forget the first time I heard that name.

The rain continued to fall, the windshield wipers beating a steady rhythm. His father drove slowly, carefully, watching the road unwind before him, lost in thought, troubled but trying not to show it. Young Michael shivered, staring at the man next to him, his eyes accusing him, but also studying this hero turned monster.

When the car had rolled into the garage, Papa shut off the engine; through a window they could see their home. Michael sensed that his father felt what he felt: that they had changed, both of them. That going in that house would mean something different, now.

The boy asked, "Does Mama know?"

His father replied, "Mama knows that I love Mr. Rooney like a father. When we had nothing, he gave us a home. A life. We owe him. Do you understand?"

Michael nodded. "Yes."

"Come on inside."

The boy had been worried about what they would say to Mama, but she and Peter weren't back from the concert yet. The concert had slipped his mind—real life, day-to-day activity, the little things that made up a normal world . . . the boy had forgotten all about the wonderful ordinary life he'd been living. Could he go back to that life? Could life ever be normal? Could he be an ordinary boy again?

All Michael Sullivan, Jr., wanted to do was crawl in his warm bed, between comforter and covers, where it would be toasty and safe.

His father looked in on him, but did not tuck him in. All he said was good night, from the doorway.

Michael managed a g'nite, and tried to go to sleep, thinking he would right away, as tired as he was.

But sleep did not come. Life wasn't that easy, anymore. And he lay awake, hands balled into fists outside the covers, as he stared up at the ceiling, the

weather reflecting weirdly, projecting strange drift-
ing shapes he couldn't make out. He wasn't sure he
wanted to, but he couldn't stop looking at them.

In the garage Michael Sullivan, Sr., cleaned and
oiled the disassembled parts of his Thompson submachine gun—a weapon made for the Great War in
which he'd fought, but developed too late for the
trench action it was made for. He got grease on his
hands and wiped them off with a cloth—seemed to
take an inordinate amount of time, tonight, to get his
hands clean.

Methodically, with ritualistic care, he packed
away the parts of the machine gun into his plush-
padded black carrying case. He stowed the case in
the cupboard, with its ammunition drums, and
locked away the tools of his trade.

But he did not go back into the house, not immediately. He stood there staring at the closed cupboard, deep in thought, lost in the possible
ramifications of what had transpired—worried for
his son and the boy's emotional welfare, and most of
all concerned about the safety of them all.

Connor Rooney was an unstable, dangerous man.

And if Connor's father weren't John Rooney,
Michael Sullivan would have gone back out into the
rainy, snowy night and killed that homicidal lunatic,
to protect his family and himself.

But in a strange way, Connor Rooney was family,
too—a brother of sorts. And John Rooney—who, despite the wicked business they were in, was a kind,

generous, benevolent soul—loved Michael Sullivan and Annie and especially their boys. Sullivan knew this with as much certainty as he knew there was a God, a heaven, and a hell.

Yet even the most pious man, in silence, alone at night, can have doubts.

At breakfast the next morning, Michael, Peter, and their mother were already at the table when their father entered, joining them. Annie smiled at her husband, but he seemed distracted, his attention—his rather somber gaze—directed at their oldest boy, who seemed to be avoiding that gaze.

Yet she sensed no anger in either of them.

Confused, Annie said to Michael, "Will you clear your plate, Michael?"

"I'll do it later."

"It's time for school now, just—"

The boy worked up a shrug—it seemed to take all his energy. "It's only a plate."

Amazed, Annie looked at her husband for support; his eyes dropped to the table. What was going on? This wasn't like Michael—the words did not have a smart-aleck tone to them, nothing really overtly disrespectful; more like he was listless, that he somehow just didn't care. . . .

But before this could turn into a confrontation— or not—the honk of a car horn outside the kitchen window drew everyone's attention away from the breakfast table.

Recognizing Mr. Rooney's horn, Michael rose and walked from the table and out the front door.

Peter followed after his brother.

Annie, still seated at the table, watched with interest as her husband got up and went to the window. She rose and joined him—the sight a common one, the fancy Pierce-Arrow pulling up before their house, the driver stopping, John Rooney stepping out of the back just in time to catch Peter, who hurled himself into the old man's arms for a hug Rooney cheerfully delivered.

Annie stood close to her husband at the window, noting his oddly glazed expression as he took in what would normally be a cheery sight.

"What's he doing here?" she asked.

Sullivan looked for the words. "Michael was hiding in the car last night when I went out."

"Oh, Jesus, Michael . . ."

"I've spoken to him. It won't happen again."

She started to say something, and he turned to her, his face a stony mask. His eyes told her: *no questions—we won't speak of this.*

And he left her side, heading to the front closet for his topcoat and hat.

Outside, Mr. Rooney had wandered over to where young Michael was climbing on his bike.

"Just the feller!" the old man said, pointing a curled finger at Michael. Then Mr. Rooney sidled up to the boy on the bike and said surreptitiously, "Our secret, right?"

Michael pulled back, alarmed.

Mr. Rooney frowned. "I'm talking about the dice." He held out a shiny coin. "A man of honor always pays his debts."

Reluctantly the boy took the dollar.

Mr. Rooney stood so close, the grown-up smells smothered the crisp morning air—cigar smoke, liquor, coffee.

"And keeps his word," the old man told the boy, something hard in the ice-blue eyes, something Michael had never seen, or at least noticed, before.

"I'm gonna be late for school," Michael said, and pedaled off, the old man watching him go. The boy could feel the eyes on his back, burning holes.

When Rooney turned, his man Sullivan was heading out of the house, shrugging into his topcoat. The wife, Annie, was in the window—she looked concerned. The old man threw her a friendly smile and a wave as her husband got into the back of the Pierce-Arrow. She waved back, but Rooney could tell his gesture had done little to assuage her unease.

Within ten minutes, Rooney and Sullivan were having coffee, seated across from each other in a comfortable pub in downtown Rock Island. A glorified diner, the place did a brisk business, and was crowded with breakfast trade—of course, a number of the patrons were Rooney bodyguards. Several more burly boyos were stationed out on the sidewalk.

Day after a dustup like last night, the old man knew, extra precautions were called for.

Rooney said, "How's Michael? Is he okay?"

Sullivan seemed happy—or was it relieved?—to hear these words. He said, "I've spoken to him. He understands."

Nodding, Rooney said, "It's tough . . . seeing that for the first time."

Sullivan paused—probably thinking about his own first exposure to the like, Rooney knew.

"Well," the old man said, and he bestowed a smile of warmth upon his loyal lieutenant, "you turned out."

Sullivan didn't smile, however; his eyes had a haunted quality that disturbed Rooney.

Boys will be boys, Rooney thought. *Who hadn't played stowaway as a whelp?* "You can't protect children forever. If it wasn't this, it would've been something else."

Sullivan said nothing.

Rooney waved at a waitress for the check, saying, "It's natural law—sons are put on this earth to trouble their fathers."

Sullivan smiled, and Rooney felt relief: the boy still loved him.

6

*When my father was working for Rooney, I never knew
the old man was an attorney. But in fact John Rooney did
study law and was admitted to the Illinois bar. Soon the
fledgling attorney began to make powerful associates in
the world of business and politics. Nothing criminal,
nothing shady, had yet emerged in the life of this ambi-
tious young man, who even ran as a Democrat for the
State Legislature.*

*But when he lost that election, an embittered Rooney
began to establish his own form of government.*

*And over the next decades, he assembled a criminal or-
ganization that gathered enormous tribute from any and
all activities that were in conflict with the laws of the time.*

*With or without politics, sanctioned by society or not,
John Rooney would rule from his roost on the bluff.*

Michael Sullivan, Sr., stayed in the shadows. John
Rooney, seated at the head of a long table, had his
back to Sullivan, who had a good view of most
everyone else at this meeting of the Rooney version

of a board of directors. The confab was taking place in the grand parlor of the mansion, a room filled not long ago with partying mourners, only a few of whom were included in this esteemed company, the Chief of Police a prime example. Another was a snappily dressed Connor Rooney, seated at his father's left hand.

The gathering included delegates of the various arms of the Rooney empire—eight men representing distilleries, casinos, brothels, loan-sharking, extortion. This had been a working supper—coffee, drinks, the remainder of meals on plates, were in as much evidence as papers and file folders—and was now winding down, as night worked its way in the windows.

Jimmy and Sean, two of Rooney's prime bruiser bodyguards, were on the door; but the great man's back could only be trusted to Mike Sullivan, who sat against the wall, a drink on a small table beside him. The Rooney family's chief enforcer did not like to think of himself as a glorified bodyguard, but in some respects, on some occasions, he was that very thing. Most of the men at this table had taken individual meetings throughout the day with John Rooney; and after last night's warehouse debacle, Sullivan had been primed and ready for retaliation.

Nothing so far, from the McGovern forces; and many of the meetings today had been designed to unruffle feathers and smooth the way for a nonviolent transition. But the empty chair at the table—Fin McGovern's seat, which no one had dared take—

provided an eloquent wordless reminder of the damage that had been done.

Speaking at the moment was Joe Kelly—in his fifties, the fleshily prosperous-looking partner in Rooney's law firm. Kelly spoke authoritatively. "John has made it clear that Fin McGovern's operation will be divided up locally among two territories that John will select personally." With a less than subtle nod toward the empty chair of Fin McGovern, Kelly added, "I'd like to take this moment to thank our friend Mr. Rance for interrupting a busy travel schedule to pay us a visit."

Kelly gestured across the table to Rance, a fussy little man in his forties, his clothes well tailored, his grooming immaculate; the man had already made a to-do about having to have a whole slice of lemon in his tea. Rance, in the company of Kelly, had met with Rooney this afternoon, a meeting surprisingly short for such an important man to have rearranged his schedule to accommodate it.

"Thank you, Joe," Rance said.

Rance was, after all, the financial adviser and one of the top accountants of the Capone organization, second only to Jake "Greasy Thumb" Guzik himself. And while Guzik represented the old breed, Rance was the future.

Though he'd been sitting there throughout the meeting, Rance exchanged nods and polite introductions with everyone at the table, but otherwise allowing the lawyer to carry the ball.

Adjusting his wire rims, and with his eyes on

Rooney, Kelly said to the assemblage, "Mr. Rance met with John and I earlier to make another bid for our involvement in the unions. . . ."

Nods and frowns and chuckles greeted this observation, which was hardly stop-the-presses news.

Sullivan wondered why Mr. Rance wasn't speaking for himself.

Perhaps the reason was John Rooney, whose voice boomed from the head of the table. "And I told Mr. Rance what I told him before. What men do after work has made us rich." That included Mr. Rance and their friends in Chicago, Rooney pointed out. Men liked to drink, men liked to place a bet, men liked to wench . . . and they paid the Rooney organization dearly for the privilege. "We don't need to screw 'em at work, as well."

Kelly quickly said that he'd wrapped up what he had to discuss, adding, "Any other business . . . John?"

Rooney was staring at the empty chair. Then, without looking at his son, the old man said, "Yes. Connor—do you want to say something about last night?"

And now John Rooney turned his eyes toward his boy—Sullivan could not see the gaze, from where he stood, but in his mind's eye he saw it vividly: blue ice eyes, a face as blank as a slate, but ready for rage to be written on it.

Yet the son—who clearly hadn't planned on speaking on this subject, as unprepared as a kid in class with a surprise test sprung on him—said, awkwardly, with a touch of laughter in his tone, "Well . . . I'd like to apologize for what happened. Especially to you, Pa—two wakes in a month—what can I say?" Connor's creepy grin spread across his face.

The grand parlor went deathly still.

John Rooney's face was long and pale, his eyes glittering with anger. "We lost a good man last night." His head swiveled toward his son and his stare would have turned Lot's wife to salt as surely as Sodom and Gomorrah. "You think it's *funny*? Try again."

Connor, already shaken, did his best to maintain a shred of dignity. He said, without laughter, but so quietly it was difficult to hear, "I'd like to apologize for what I did—"

Rooney cut his son off at the legs this time, slamming his hand down on the table. "You'd *like* to apologize? *Try again.*"

Silence draped the room, a shroud of humiliation worn by Connor, but uneasily felt by all of them except old man Rooney himself. Much as he despised Connor for what he had done last night, Sullivan felt bad for the man, who now pushed his chair away from the table, got to his feet, head hanging, a disobedient child shamed before his peers.

"Gentlemen," Connor said, "my apologies."

Face flushed, Connor was looking nowhere, trembling under his father's censure. Anger would come later—right now it was all the man could do to hold back tears.

"Is everyone clear about bit-borrowers?" Kelly

asked, breaking the tension. "There are far too many debts outstanding."

Connor, let off the hook, remained glazed, silent.

In response to Kelly's question, Rooney spoke to the man behind him, saying simply, "Mike?"

"Just give me the names," Sullivan said. "Tell me who to visit."

After a beat, Rooney rose to his feet. "Thank you, gentleman," he said, dismissing those around the table. He turned to Sullivan and said, "Come on upstairs."

"Sure."

As the men stood, gathering their papers, Rooney went to Sullivan, slipped an arm around his shoulder; the old man, his manner as warm as it was familiar, walked Sullivan out of the grand parlor, toward the stairs. His voice was affectionate, respectful as he spoke of his "angel" winging his way to nudge misguided souls into righteousness.

Connor Rooney, the only man still seated at the table, watched this bitterly. The men in this room—men who one day would be under his command—had seen his father disrespect him, and treat with favor that gunman, Sullivan.

When the room had emptied, Connor sat alone, deep in thought, lost in the twisted passages of his mind.

Less than an hour later, after meeting with Rooney in his study, Sullivan strolled to his Ford, parked in the driveway near the Pierce-Arrow.

Sullivan had reached his car and was just about to drive away when he heard Connor's voice, surprisingly cheerful, calling out, "Mike!"

He turned and Connor trotted up to him. "Dad forgot to give you this—reminder for Tony Calvino. He's light again."

Connor handed Sullivan the sealed envelope with Calvino's name scrawled on it.

Sullivan asked, "You coming?"

Strangely sheepish, Connor said, "Nah. . . . I'm under house arrest for a while. . . . Look, I am sorry. 'Bout last night. I was . . . you know."

Connor seemed genuinely regretful about the trouble he'd caused. Both men knew that Connor should have watched his mouth around a proud, grieving man like McGovern.

Sullivan said, "All right."

Connor tossed him a wave and headed back into the mansion. The guy seemed in an awfully forgiving mood for someone who'd been humiliated by his own father not so long ago.

Of course, a lot of Connor's actions could be explained by one fact, Sullivan knew: the bastard was crazy as a bedbug.

On the Iowa side of the river, given over to sin of varying stripes, Bucktown nestled in the riverfront blocks of Davenport's west side. The wide-open area—where it was said you could buy anything for a buck—resided mostly in Tony Calvino's pocket. This seedy, trashy district was not Sullivan's favorite part of the world; he parked his Ford on the street, ignoring the devil-red glow of the CALVINO'S neon, walking around to the alley entrance.

Tony Calvino had once been a contender in local rackets, and Bucktown remained his stronghold. But Calvino had a reputation for indulging in his own merchandise—from booze to dames to drugs—and that had reduced him to just another acolyte of John Rooney.

Breath smoking in the cold, Sullivan moved down a stairway to a basement door, next to which a wooden sign read SUBWAY POOL AND BILLIARDS. A size forty-eight bouncer in a size forty-four suit stood guard at the door, arms folded, rocking on his heels; a small kerosene heater kept the air warm. He had the bored, self-confident look of a guy who had beaten the crap out of countless others.

"Help you, sir?" the bouncer said with a faint lilt of sarcasm. Sullivan, in his dark suit and topcoat, must have seemed like another slumming business-man. "Or just lookin'?"

"Come to see Mr. Calvino," he said.

"Yeah, and who are you?"

"Mike Sullivan."

The bouncer stopped rocking on his heels; his eyes widened and his complexion paled as the blood in his face ran for cover. "Oh . . . yes, sir."

The guy was reaching for the doorknob when Sullivan asked quietly, "You don't want to frisk me?"

The bouncer blinked. "Should I?"

"It's a good idea."

The bouncer gave Sullivan a quick pat down,

found the .45 in the shoulder holster, and stuck the pistol in his own waistband, under his suitcoat, with an apologetic shrug.

"That's the only one," Sullivan assured him.

Then the bouncer—flustered and friendly—led the way through the pool hall beyond the door; in a room awash with green-felt tables under pools of light from conical hanging lamps, no one was playing right now. Tumbleweed might have blown through.

The heavy door opened, revealing a bright bustling casino area, unleashing the near-hysterical sounds of laughter and dismay, roulette balls spinning, dealers calling out cards, dice clicking against wood. For the most part, however, the patrons here were not high-hat high rollers, just workingmen with their girlfriends or maybe even their wives, or somebody else's wife, risking money they were lucky to be making in these hard times.

A giddy group of little boys and girls—children!— were playing ring-around-the-rosy with some slot machines, getting in the way as the two men moved through the gambling hall. It sickened Sullivan, seeing children around this vice.

The bouncer almost had to yell to be heard over the brass. "I mean, I'm a grown man and this place is getting to me. Every night there's trouble. Nobody's got no dough, but all the world's here wasting it. Always money for frills and twists, never money for food. . . . Sometimes I despair of the species, you know?"

Sullivan said nothing.

Moving to the next circle of hell, a door opened onto the receiving area of Calvino's brothel, where low-key lighting didn't soften the reddish velvet drapes and black-and-red flocked wallpaper, the air ripe with the smell of cheap perfume and face powder. Ranging from their late teens to their early thirties, soiled doves in overstuffed chemises on overstuffed settees perched and preened along the walls, like a buffet line of sex, working stiffs, and men of means alike moving down each row, picking out their selections.

At the door, the madam, a hussy in her fifties with troweled-on makeup, called out a number—"Number twelve in the beauty parlor. Who's the lucky face?"—and the girl who'd been chosen stood to receive the arm of the patron who'd picked her. With a smile worth every penny, the blonde floozy led her salesman-looking fellow down a dim corridor, and the bouncer and Sullivan followed after.

"I'm not from here," the chatty bouncer rambled on. "Things bein' what they are—jobs ain't hangin' off of trees."

The hooker and her john ducked into a cubicle, shutting a velvet drape over the doorless doorway; the entire corridor was lined with such curtained doorways, and as the two men passed by, the muffled music of sexual intercourse—funny, Sullivan noted, how remarkably similar the sounds of pleasure and pain were—provided a backdrop for the bouncer's endless chitchat.

"I'm a boxer by trade—nine consecutive titles. A record for South Orange. I'd make a real good body-guard, I think."

Sullivan remained mute as they moved down another corridor, at the dead end of which was a door.

"What I'm saying is," the bouncer said, "is Mr. Rooney looking for anyone . . . anyone like me, for example? Any chance you could ask him?"

"Sure."

A big grin broke out on the bouncer's mug. "Thank you. I appreciate that, Mr. Sullivan."

Aglow, the bouncer knocked on the door and stepped inside without waiting to be summoned.

Sullivan, alone in the hallway, pressed his ear to the door and heard the following exchange:

"Mr. Calvino . . . Mike Sullivan's here."

Calvino's husky baritone, slightly slurred, responded, "Aaah, shit. . . . Is he packing?"

Pride colored the bodyguard's voice. "Not anymore."

Sullivan smiled as he listened.

Then Calvino's voice: "All right—show him in . . . but you stick around, okay?"

Sullivan's eyes narrowed—a drawer opened; he heard something, a faint but unmistakable clunk on wood, and the rustle of paper, like a magazine.

Then the bodyguard emerged, smiling, friendly, and showed him into the office.

Sullivan went in, surprised by how slovenly the office was—boxes were stacked precariously against wallpaper-peeling walls, newspapers and ledger books lay piled on top of file cabinets. Framed portraits of Louis Armstrong and other jazz greats who'd played Calvino's hung on one wall, at varying askew angles.

And behind the big desk was the man who at one time had been John Rooney's only real competition in the Tri-Cities: Anthony Calvino, his dark suit and colorful tie a wrinkled mess, though not as much a mess as he was. Calvino was a big dark man, once a powerful person in every sense; now his rheumy eyes—and the sickeningly sweet smell of opium smoke—told another story.

On the big man's cluttered desk, in front of him, was a girlie magazine, *PEP*, folded open, tented there, as if he'd been interrupted reading. Papers and paperweights alike were jiggling on the desk, and the framed photos on the wall were shimmying. The office shared a wall with the bar, it seemed—the loud jazz music was bleeding through, sending a slight reverberation through the room. Any boss other than the drug-addled Tony Calvino would have minded; Calvino probably hadn't noticed.

Without rising, the fleshy Calvino held open his hands and beamed, as if he and Sullivan were dear old friends, not adversary acquaintances.

"Hey, how the hell are you? . . . Things good with the old man?"

They did not shake hands.

Sullivan said, "Uh-huh."

"What brings you here? Don't imagine it's the pussy."

Sullivan shook his head.

Calvino began running through a litany of his problems . . . goddamn overhead, grease for the cops and politicians . . . the Iowa side's no picnic, y'know. But didn't he always render "under" Caesar?

"I have a letter from Mr. Rooney." Sullivan's hand lifted toward his suitcoat, and Calvino and the bodyguard flinched.

But both Calvino and the bodyguard watched, tense and intent, as Sullivan reached under his topcoat into his suit jacket pocket. And when he withdrew the sealed letter, the two men visibly sighed in relief . . . which amused Sullivan, some. Reputation did have its benefits.

Calvino took the envelope, asking, "Am I behind again?" As he reached for a letter opener—which jumped with the jazz beat on his desktop—the king of Bucktown asked, "Am I in trouble?"

"I don't know. . . ."

Sullivan glanced at the tented magazine; was something under there?

Calvino unfolded the letter and read. His brow furrowed. Confused, he scratched his chin. Then his features went blank.

As the walls reverberated with the frantic music next door—"Muskrat Ramble," at the moment—the objects, the papers on the desk, continued to do a little dance . . . and from beneath the tented magazine, something black and metallic peeked.

Calvino was holding the letter in his left hand, studying it, thinking, thinking . . . then he looked up at the bodyguard with a smile, but his eyes flicked towards Sullivan.

Perhaps if the fleshy Bucktown monarch hadn't been a hophead, he'd have moved fast enough; probably not—the man merely shifted in his chair, his hand inching only a fraction when Sullivan reached under that magazine and grabbed the cold metal of the revolver there, hand finding the grip, finger finding the trigger, and as the openmouthed Calvino stared at him, the whites of his eyes as big as his pupils were small, Sullivan squeezed off one round—on the downbeat of the music, right into the gangster's forehead.

Calvino flopped onto the desk, his head hitting first, scattering everything, everywhere.

Sullivan had already turned to face the friendly bodyguard, who was fumbling for the gun in his waistband, Sullivan's own .45; but the man knew it was useless, even as he went for the weapon.

One bullet was all the job reference Mike Sullivan would ever give Calvino's ex-employee—the burly bouncer bounced against the wall, almost in time to the music, sliding down just as "Muskrat Ramble" came to a big finish.

Sullivan paused, waiting to see if anyone came charging into the room—but the raucous music had apparently covered the gunshots.

Alive but confused, wondering what had prompted

Calvino to turn on him, Sullivan looked at the desk, where the letter lay discarded by its dead recipient.

Sullivan snatched up the missive he'd delivered, which consisted of one simple, boldly scrawled sentence.

KILL SULLIVAN AND ALL DEBTS ARE PAID.

A sudden realization gripped him—he knew he'd been sent on this mission for two reasons: to meet his death—and to draw him away from his family.

Sullivan had been one target.

But Connor Rooney would have another target.

"Michael," he gasped, and he reached for the phone on the dead man's desk.

.

7

*The great unanswered question, after all these years, re-
mains: was the betrayal of Mike Sullivan the work of
Connor Rooney alone? What role, if any, did John
Rooney himself play in the treachery?*

*Strangely, my father never spoke of this—to me, at
least. But there was no doubt that that night forever
changed my father—forever changed us both.*

Troubled as she'd been the last few days—as disturbed as she was about whatever her son Michael
might have seen the night before—Annie Sullivan
could still laugh. Or at least Peter could make her
laugh.

Mother and son were in the bathroom upstairs.
This was one of those ordinary yet precious moments that she did not take for granted: a year from
now, if not sooner, her youngest son would be uncomfortable having his mother help him bathe. He
was really already too old for it, she knew; but to

her, Peter was still her baby, even though he'd turned ten.

The child liked a hot bath, and the room was steamy, the mirrors fogged. She had told him to get out, now, that he was getting all pruney, and he'd splashed water at her, and she'd leaned over the edge, splashing him back—but the boy wasn't much dissuaded by that.

In fact, he seemed to find it very funny that his mother would be silly enough to splash somebody who was already dripping wet, and his childish laughter rang in the enclosed space. The little boy's infectious glee had caught her, and as she held out a towel for him, and he stepped out over the high edge of the tub into the towel and her drying embrace, they were both still giggling.

The door cracked open, giving them a glimpse of an adult male figure in a topcoat in the dark hall.

Oh—it was the man of the house, she thought, smiling, as she toweled off her son.

But when the door opened wide, the figure there—in a dark topcoat and a knit stocking mask, balaclava style—was not her husband.

Terrified, Annie drew Peter closer. The eyes in the knit mask were blinking—the intruder seemed almost as afraid as she felt.

But the man in the knit mask raised his right arm, revealing the long-nosed revolver in his gloved hand.

Annie turned her back and put herself in front of her child, but the gun in the trembling grasp of the intruder barked once, a terrible explosion in the small room that had not finished echoing in her ears when the bullet in her heart ended her life.

Peter wasn't looking when the intruder fired the second shot.

Peter Sullivan tumbled into his mother's lifeless arms, and their blood ran together as one on the white tile floor, making crimson pools, the towel a puddle of white flecked with red.

So much for my little squealer, Connor Rooney thought. Such bravado was at odds with his trembling gun-in-hand, unaware that he had shot the wrong Sullivan boy.

After an evening of pin-the-tail-on-the-donkey, and several plates of birthday cake, Michael Sullivan, Jr., was pedaling home from St. Pete's. Tonight was clear and cold, and his breath was pluming as he tooled his bike down the street.

He'd had a long day, and kind of a lousy one—all the cake in the world couldn't make up for what he'd been through at school today. At school, in lunch, an older boy had made a crack about Papa working for "that gangster Rooney," and Michael had lost control, punching, kicking, pummeling the kid. Neither boy had been the victor, and both stayed after school.

Michael's hand was still sore from writing I WILL NOT FIGHT WITH OTHER BOYS on the blackboard, a hundred times.

He was nearly home, just gliding into the drive-

way, when he heard the harsh crack. At first he
didn't know what it was—a car backfiring maybe?
But the noise had seemed to come from inside the
house, and when he looked in that direction, a flash
in the bathroom window, on the second floor, was
accompanied by a second harsh crack . . .

. . . and he had heard similar sounds, last night,
hadn't he? *Could those have been gunshots?*

He abandoned his bike in the drive and ran toward the house, with no thought of the danger, or
what this might mean; all the eleven-year-old knew
was that his mother and his brother were in that
house! Was Papa home, too? He hadn't noticed
whether the car was in the garage. . . .

These and a dozen other frantic thoughts tumbled through the boy's brain as he ran up on the
front porch, and he was about to rush inside when
the figure of a man appeared in the glass of the
front door.

Michael froze: the man wore one of those stocking masks, but the boy thought he recognized the
figure—wasn't that . . . and the man pulled off the
mask and confirmed Michael's suspicion: *Connor
Rooney.*

Who seemed to be staring right at Michael!

Michael wanted to run, but his feet wouldn't re-
spond; and then, suddenly, he realized Uncle Connor couldn't see him—the man was fixing his hair
and seemed to be trying to compose himself before
going outside. Then the boy understood: with the
lights on in the house, Connor couldn't see Michael

.

standing out in the darkness—what Connor was doing was looking at his own reflection!

And now the man was reaching for the doorknob.

Michael plastered himself to the side of the house, so that when the door opened, he'd be tucked behind it.

Which was exactly what happened. Uncle Connor didn't notice him there, door open wide. The man stood on the porch on unsteady feet and fished a hip flask from inside his topcoat. He took a healthy swig.

Then, leaving the door wide open, Connor Rooney tottered off into the night.

When Uncle Connor had gone, Michael came out from behind the door and just stood there on the porch, staring at the open doorway for a long, long time.

He knew this had to be bad. The sick feeling in his stomach was only partly all that cake he'd eaten at St. Pete's. Maybe Uncle Connor had been here to do business with Papa; but Mama had said his father would be late, that he had to go do something for Mr. Rooney.

And those noises had sounded like the gunshots at that warehouse last night.

If something bad had happened in the house, he knew he should help—he should be running in there, at top speed; but he was a kid, and afraid, and perhaps he knew, instinctively, that if something bad had indeed happened, due to that crazy man he'd just seen leave, there would be no help he could give.

But Michael finally went in. The house was strangely still—the ticking of clocks, some dripping of faucets, nothing more. A droning sound turned out to be the phone—it was off the hook in the hall. He thought about putting the receiver back in place, but didn't. Nearby the stairs yawned endlessly—and at the top, steam from the bathroom floated like fog, but other smoke was mingled there, too. He'd seen such smoke last night.

Guns had made it.

Trembling, he moved up the stairs. In his mind he was running; but the reality was, he'd never climbed them more slowly. At the top, he turned and headed down the corridor to the bathroom.

He went in.

His instincts had proven right: there was nothing he could have done. His mother and his brother lay sprawled lifelessly, eyes open, but with no more expression than marbles; they'd both been shot in the chest. Pools of blood glistened. The faucet dripped. The mirror was fogged up. They were dead.

The boy backed out of the bathroom, a sleep-walker caught in a bad dream, and moved down the hall, and down the stairs. Still in his trance, he found himself in the dining room. His mother had left his plate on the table, the food spoiled, all nasty and crusty; he had told Mama he'd clean it off later, and she had left it for him, to show him. Teach him a lesson.

Michael cleared the plate off into the trash, then went to the sink to run water on it. Like his mother had requested. Lesson learned.

Then he returned to the table and sat there. He folded his hands, like when saying grace. The boy knew not to call the police; it was not what Papa would have wanted. And he was still sitting there when his father flew into the house, through the front door, his big pistol from the war in hand.

Sullivan—unable to raise the family on the phone, knowing he could call neither anyone associated with John Rooney nor the police—had broken every speed law getting here, hurtling across city streets, passing traffic on the government bridge, earning outraged honks and curses from other drivers, and barely noticing.

He said nothing to his son, who was sitting at the table, dazed.

He took the stairs three at a time, and ran until the terrible sight stopped him at the bathroom doorway. "No!" Michael heard his father scream out. The husband went to his wife, knelt beside her, touched her throat where a pulse should be; then the father did the same for his youngest boy. Finally, he stood, turned off the harsh overhead light, so they could sleep better, and he went out into the hall.

He leaned a hand against the wall, and then slid to the floor and sat there crying, gun beside him, his head in his hands. He had lost everything. Everything.

Michael was there now, standing over his father as he wept.

At Connor Rooney's apartment, John Rooney stood over his son, who sat at his desk, distressed. The room was in some disarray from the father hurling the son to the floor.

"I'm sorry," Connor was saying. "I'm sorry. . . ."

His father demanded over and over again why he had done this thing. "You stupid!"

"The kid would've talked . . . I'm sorry."

The old man exploded with rage, excoriating his son for his stupidity, and his cowardice, and then— apparently unable to verbalize his rage, much less satisfy it—the old man began to slap his son, striking him, forcing him to his knees.

"You stupid little . . ." And the old man began to rage. "Goddamn you! I curse the day you were born . . . I curse it . . . I curse it. . . ."

He continued to rave and rant—his son had brought him nothing but disappointment and shame, he should have drowned him like a goddamn cat.

And finally John Rooney, exhausted, an emotional wreck himself, fell to his knees, beside his son, as if they were both praying. Connor was breathing hard, and blubbering like a baby.

And then the old man embraced his boy and soothed him, patting his back, there there, there there. . . . "My boy . . ."

*   *   *

Sullivan told his son to go to his room and pack his things. They had to leave.

Michael swallowed and nodded.

The boy went to the bedroom he'd shared with his brother. He packed his clothes, and a few toys and the Big Little Books he hadn't read yet.

When Papa closed the front door, it was almost a slam—there was something final about it, the boy thought.

Papa went into the garage and came back a few minutes later with the black hard-shell case in hand—the tommy gun would be making the trip with them, and somehow Michael was glad.

Before they got into the car, Michael paused, looking back at the house he'd been raised in—he'd never lived anywhere else. He'd even been born there, in his parents' bedroom, where Mama lay now.

His father touched his shoulder. "That's not our home anymore," he reminded the boy. "It's just an empty building."

With their suitcases in the backseat, his father's big one and Michael's small one, and the black hard-shell carrying case as well, his father drove at a normal speed through the residential streets of Rock Island. Within ten minutes they were downtown, and Papa pulled the car into a parking space, where the shadows were dark.

Across the street a neon sign glowed: FLORENCE HOTEL. "Stay here. Stay out of sight," Sullivan said.

But when his father began to go, Michael grabbed on to his arm, holding him back.

Michael had never seen the look in his father's eyes before—his expression was apologetic, and also sad. Papa's eyes were red, as if he'd been crying.

"Michael, tomorrow they'll realize we're gone and come after us. I have to protect you now."

"Please, Pa!" Michael couldn't see how his father leaving him alone was any kind of protection at all!

His father sat there—thinking, almost like he was fighting with himself. Then he reached in his left-hand topcoat pocket and removed a small gun—a revolver with a very short barrel—and handed it to Michael. "Here, take this."

But the boy couldn't make his fist unclench.

"Take it. Take it, boy."

"No! No! I don't want it."

His father gently yet firmly opened his son's fingers and placed the gun into his palm.

Papa warned Michael that he might hear things—shouts, a gunshot or two—but to sit tight. "It's got six shots."

"If I'm not back in half an hour, go to Reverend Lynch at First Methodist and tell him what happened. . . . *Don't* go to Father Callaway."

Michael didn't understand—that was a Protestant church! Why not go to St. Pete's and Father Callaway?

Quietly his father told him that Rooney money built that church . . . and sent Father Callaway to

Rome last summer to meet the Pope. They would find no sanctuary there.

Michael said nothing, looking down at his hand, where the small gun seemed so big. . . .

Papa, about to open the door, paused and his eyes held the boy—as if he were memorizing Michael's features—then slipped out into the night, moving down the sidewalk.

In the shadows of a recessed doorway across from the Florence Hotel, Sullivan watched as men outside the building milled about, cars parked in front, more cars arriving, a small crowd of Rooney thugs growing bigger as the group readied themselves to go after him. If any confirmation was needed, the brave talk among the strutting men occasionally contained the name "Sullivan" and the word "Angel."

Soon Rooney's former chief enforcer—hearing the sounds of cars starting up, heading off, the search party leaving—was in the alley behind the hotel. No one back here, somewhat surprisingly; he began to climb the fire escape cautiously, .45 in one hand.

At the second-floor landing, he looked in the window at an empty corridor; he forced the window open and stepped quietly in, all the while looking for an armed watchdog, but seeing no one. He walked down the hall to the doorway to Connor Rooney's apartment; the lower edge of the door revealed the lights on in there. His first thought was to kick the door in, but that would be too loud.

He tried the doorknob—and the door swung open!

Walking in, gun raised, he found himself in a dark room, staring at the back of a well-dressed, self-composed Joe Kelly, seated in the middle of the room, in a comfortable chair, before a coffee table. The portly, prosperous-looking lawyer seemed to have been waiting for the Rooney lieutenant to appear. He placed a briefcase on the table in front of him.

Sullivan shut the door, and—looking all around the well-appointed apartment—kept the .45 poised to shoot as he told John Rooney's long-time law partner, "I don't have any business with you, Mr. Kelly."

Genial, pleasant, the attorney held his hands open, palms up. "Ah, but I have business with you, Mike. I'm here as Mr. Rooney's representative." He shifted in his chair; he was walking a tightrope between keeping this friendly and yet serious. He said he was here to let Sullivan know that John Rooney had nothing to do with the unfortunate—might he even say *tragic*—steps taken against the man's family. All of this had been Connor Rooney's own doing, a deplorable thing . . . and an unauthorized action.

Then, Sullivan said, Mr. Rooney would understand why he had to kill Connor.

Kelly sighed and his expression was suitably somber. He shifted in the chair again.

Sullivan said nothing.

"What's that?" Sullivan asked, pointing to the briefcase.

"It's twenty-five thousand dollars, Mike. Mr. Rooney wants you to know there's more if you want it. . . ."

The disgust in Sullivan's face revealed what he thought of the offer. Money . . . always money. . . .

The lawyer shook his head again, acknowledging the lamentable circumstances. "Mike, you have friends in Ireland. Why don't you take Peter and leave?"

"I can't take Peter. He's dead."

Kelly was confused, thrown. . . .

And then the lawyer realized that that fool Connor Rooney hadn't even known who he was killing.

Sullivan snapped, "Where's Connor?"

Kelly shook his head. "He's in hiding."

"*Where?*"

"You know I can't tell you that, Mike."

Sullivan raised the .45, leveling it directly at the lawyer's head.

But Kelly was an old courtroom warrior and there was steel in his eyes as he replied, "You think sticking a gun to my head is going to make a difference to me? If I tell you, I'm dead, anyway—we both are."

Sullivan thumbed back the hammer on the .45, a small click that seemed to echo in the room.

"*Think*, Mike," Kelly said, sweating but toughing it out. "Don't be stupid. . . . I'm just the messenger. . . ."

Sullivan seemed to think about this for a second, the gun in his hand sagging down as he looked at the briefcase. Sullivan had made his decision. He brought his eyes—and the gun—back up.

"Then I need you to give Mr. Rooney a message for me."

"What is it?" Kelly asked, ready to help.

And Sullivan shot the man in the head.

Teeth chattering from the cold, Michael, in the car, thought he heard a gunshot, but he wasn't sure; it sounded far away. And then before very long, his father was sliding in behind the wheel. He didn't look the same, somehow.

"Give me the gun," he said. Michael noticed the small splatters of blood on his father's hands as he reached for the pistol.

Papa said it was getting colder. The boy should take the blanket from the backseat and wrap it around himself.

Michael did, and they began to drive.

Finally Michael asked, "Where are we going?"

"To Chicago. There's a man there who runs things. I've done work for him. . . . I have to find out where he stands."

Michael thought about that. An important man in Chicago . . . It sounded mysterious. . . .

His father said, "Try to get some sleep."

Michael leaned against the door, wrapped in the blanket. Despite everything that had happened, he was so exhausted, the boy knew he would fall asleep at once. Before he did, he wondered what this important man's name was.

The name was burning in his father's mind.

Capone.

8

*Many considered the real brains behind the Capone orga-
nization to be Capone's second-in-command, Frank Nitti.
Nitti held the role of Capone's chief enforcer—the job my
father held in John Rooney's organization—and was his
heir apparent.*

*Nitti was at the fore of the new breed of gangster. He
understood that the mob was like any American big business, and that the murderous ways so ingrained in thugs
like Capone, who'd come up through the street, had to be
kept in check. Under Nitti, the so-called Chicago Outfit
would expand into legitimate businesses and, in particular, unions; the killing would continue, when necessary . . . but more discreetly.*

Sullivan drove through the night, often taking
back roads and circuitous routes on his journey to
Chicago, though he did not expect Rooney or his men
to anticipate this move. His son slumbering behind
him, Sullivan experienced a strange combination of
clarity—he was not at all tired—and a dreamlike

state. His headlights cut through darkness like search-lights, and the winter-barren farmland—some of the richest land in the United States—seemed a surrealis-tic wasteland around them.

When night began its fade to morning, light eas-ing over the endless fields, the rural landscape took on a stark reality and beauty. Annie had an eye for such things. Like any woman, she would point out colorful flowers in summer; but at this time of year, she might also draw his attention to a tree silhouet-ted against the sky like a ghostly skeleton.

The boy slept. Sullivan was thankful for that, and when Michael did finally waken, they were deep in Chicago's Loop, skyscrapers looming, safe and anonymous in the morning traffic. It must have seemed so big to the boy, his eyes wide as he looked all around at the man-made canyon walls.

The Chicago Public Library faced Michigan Av-enue between Randolph and Washington Streets. The turn-of-the-century classical-looking building was not a skyscraper, rather a massive elongated limestone structure, a fortress of knowledge. The boy would be safe there.

Before long, they were on foot, just a man in a topcoat and fedora, and a boy in a jacket and cap, in a sea of early-morning workers—businessmen, secretaries, blue-collar types—and again, Sullivan felt secure in their anonymity. He escorted his son—who he'd instructed to bring along his small suitcase—in on the building's Washington Street side, entering an immense world of glass mosaics and marble;

Michael's reaction of wonder touched the father in Sullivan, despite all he had on his mind.

He walked the boy to a huge reading room, where benches arranged in long rows were crowded with students and other scholars mingling with the down-and-out, mothers with babies, and the elderly, all just escaping the cold.

Sitting Michael down in the middle of a bench, Sullivan said, "I want you to wait here for me."

The boy's anxiety leaped into his eyes, but he merely said, "Sure."

"I won't be long. You'll be all right?"

Michael nodded.

"Good boy."

Sullivan didn't notice how much his son liked hearing that.

On his way toward the exit, Sullivan caught his reflection in a mirrored wall—he looked pretty rough, unshaven. He ducked into a bathroom and threw water on his face, ran his hands through his hair, doing his best to spruce up.

With his father gone, Michael got into his little suitcase; there, among some clothes, were his pipe, his dice, and two Big Little Books, a Tom Mix and the Lone Ranger one that he was still reading. Selecting that one, the boy sat and thumbed it open. His eyes looked at the full-page picture at right, of the Lone Ranger holding a gun on a sheriff. The caption, predictably redundant, read: "The Lone Ranger had the Sheriff covered."

Five minutes later, in the vast room, surrounded

by big-city strangers, the boy was still staring at the same page.

Then, his face blank, he shut the book, pushed it aside; he felt his lower lip begin to tremble and his eyes began to get wet, his whole face quivering, as if he had no control over it, which he didn't.

The boy wept, trying to stay quiet and not attract attention, because his father wouldn't have approved.

At Twenty-second Street and South Michigan Avenue, the Lexington had once been one of Chicago's most elite hotels, and the fourteen-floor structure still made an impressive appearance, with its turreted corners and bay windows. Sullivan had been here before—also at the former mob headquarters, the Metropole Hotel, just a block away. The Capone organization had the run of the place, controlling the third, fourth, and fourteenth floors and scattered rooms throughout, many of the latter taken up by the numerous hookers and showgirls Capone kept salted away for the convenience of himself and his boys.

Standing across the street, eyes on the marble pillars framing the entrance, Sullivan knew full well he was entering a mob stronghold. Capone had put in alarms, moving walls, hidden panels, and Christ knew how many other security measures. Though the hotel looked normal enough—doormen and bellboys thronged the glass doorways—the lobby would be crawling with Outfit gunmen. Nonetheless, as an expression of good faith, he was unarmed, the .45 and his other weapons left behind in the parked Ford. All Sullivan had on his side was the unexpected boldness of what he was about to do—that, and his reputation.

Moments later, Sullivan was walking through the magnificent lobby, across the black-and-white-checkered tile floor toward the iron-grille elevators. One of those elevators—which no one seemed to be using—stood vacant, while on either side of it, two watchdogs in Maxwell Street suits stood guard.

The brawnier of the two, Harry, leaned against a wall, reading *The Racing News.* The other one, Marco—taller, skinnier—was smoking a cigarette, rocking on his feet, eyeing the floozies who were a part of the odd Lexington mix that included a surprising share of legitimate guests—salesmen and other professional types in Chicago on business.

Sullivan approached them with studied casualness, saying, "Hello, fellows . . . how are you?"

Harry looked up from his racing paper, obviously startled to see this unshaven figure. "We heard what happened—how are you holding up?" said one of the watchdogs.

Not missing a beat, Sullivan said, "I need to talk to Mr. Nitti."

"He's awful busy."

"I can wait."

The two watchdogs exchanged glances; both of them knew only too well who and what Mike Sullivan was.

Harry shrugged. "Okay, take the man to the top."

Marco stepped inside the elevator and so did Sullivan.

Indicating he meant no disrespect, Marco patted Sullivan down, finding nothing. Sullivan had expected this—it was a matter of course. This was a friendly visit.

Marco swung shut the grillwork doors. Fourteen floors took a while, and they rode in strained silence, the elevator continuing on its slightly jostling course, making no stops along the way.

Then they were there, at the top floor waiting room, where politicians and businessmen of varying degrees of respectability mingled with shadier-looking figures. Cigarette smoke floated like a blue haze as the men sat and chatted, talking business and sports and even family, drinking the coffee provided thoughtfully by the Capone organization.

Everyone was settled in for a wait, and Sullivan had left his son with an hour and a half deadline. He gave the receptionist—a pleasant if officious thirty-ish woman who sat near the focal-point door marked PRIVATE—his name, acknowledged he had no appointment, but suggested she tell Mr. Nitti that Mr. Sullivan was here. Then he took a seat.

After a while, when she had not yet done as he'd asked, he settled his gaze on her, and when her eyes met his, he checked his watch and raised an eyebrow.

The receptionist got the message—though she did not recognize Sullivan, she clearly could see that he was not a part of the political/business crowd taking up the other chairs. And despite the pretense of normal business the Capone organization made, even a receptionist like this knew the score: the deadly-looking unshaven man should not be kept waiting.

She spoke to her boss on the intercom, then looked up at Sullivan and nodded.

He thanked her as she held open the door for him.

The office was spacious, a lavishly appointed executive suite worthy of LaSalle Street, all dark woodwork, with a desk and a conference table, and of course a fireplace over which hung an oil portrait of Al Capone.

Frank Nitti did not cut the imposing figure Capone did, either in the portrait or in life. A small mustached man in his mid-forties, Nitti was in his white shirtsleeves with dark suspenders, but his gray and black tie was not loosened, and there was nothing casual about the well-groomed former barber. As he approached his visitor—offering a hand, which Sullivan shook—Nitti seemed typically cordial yet distant.

"Sorry to keep you out there, Mike," Nitti said. He was smoking a cigarette held in his gesturing hand. The gangster did a fairly good job of not registering surprise at Sullivan's unshaven, rumpled appearance. "We all just heard what happened . . . Jesus, I'm sorry."

Sullivan said nothing.

"Sit down. You want some coffee?"

Sullivan shook his head, and remained standing. "Thanks for seeing me, Mr. Nitti."

Nitti told him not to be silly. Al was in Florida, holed up with his lawyers, some legal matters pending. Nitti hadn't talked to him about Sullivan's situation yet. But he was sure Al, who was after all a family man himself, would be distressed by his loss.

Sympathies expressed, Nitti's manner shifted to strictly business; they stood facing each other at a respectful distance, not far from a window that offered a commanding view of the South Side of Chicago— the Capone/Nitti empire.

Nitti asked, "So what can I do for you, Mike?"

Sullivan paused; rather formally, he said, "I would like to work for you."

That seemed to amuse Nitti; he chuckled, exhaled smoke, then said, "Well now, that's very interesting, Mike."

They both knew Sullivan was the best at what he did. That for him to join the Capone ranks, as a loyal soldier, would be a real benefit. . . .

"And in return," Sullivan continued, "I'd like you to turn a blind eye to what I have to do."

"And what's that?"

Sullivan held Nitti's gaze. "<u>Kill</u> the man who murdered my family."

The ganglord blew out more smoke. For endless seconds, he said nothing, still as stone.

Then not unkindly, Nitti reminded him that his wife and boy were already gone. "Is one more body going to make any difference?"

In Sullivan's ledger book, yes. "It's a good proposal, Mr. Nitti. I'll work only for you. You know I can do a good job."

Nitti shook his head, some frustration in his smile. "Listen, Mike—I respect you. We'd like nothing more than to have you work for us . . . but not like this."

Sullivan narrowed his eyes, not following.

"What you're asking is impossible," Nitti added with a shrug.

"Is it?"

Sullivan had said it himself—Nitti was a businessman. Much as he might personally loathe these despicable things that had been done to the man's family, the alliance between Capone and the Rooneys was a long-standing, and profitable, one.

Nitti, impatient, moved forward. "Let me explain something you may not have realized. All these years you lived under the protection of people who care for you. And those same people are trying to protect you, now. . . . Including me."

A chill passed through Sullivan's bones: *Rooney had already come to them.*

Nitti's mouth tightened, but his forehead was smooth. "But if you go ahead with this . . . if you open that door, you'll be walking through it alone. And all that trust, all that loyalty, will no longer exist for you. . . . And Mike—you won't make it. Not with a little boy."

This meeting was over.

"You're already protecting him, aren't you?" Sullivan said.

Nitti shook his head—Connor Rooney wasn't what they were protecting. "We're just protecting our interests, Mike."

Suddenly the weight of the worst hours of his life fell heavily on Sullivan's shoulders. He could not hide the distress in his voice. "I drove through the night to see you."

"I appreciate that. And now I suggest you drive yourself back—go home and bury your wife and child. With our blessing."

Sullivan slowly shook his head, then stood up. "It won't be that simple."

Sullivan turned and went out quickly, his eyes taking everything in as he moved through the reception area to where businessmen were stepping onto the elevator, Marco again playing operator. He stepped on, but then as the doors were about to be closed, thought better of it and stepped off.

Down the corridor he found the service stairs and made his way to the lobby, where he blended into the throng of the busy hotel. Though he sensed no pursuit, he knew he could no longer trust Nitti. Honor, loyalty, trust—all of those were old ideas, now.

But a new idea was forming. So this was all business, was it? Right now the Capone crowd considered the Rooney alliance a valuable asset. Sullivan aimed to change that view. He would hurt Frank

Nitti. He would make the man bleed . . . not red, but green.

When Sullivan had left the room, Frank Nitti slipped through a doorway into a small side room, where two men had been tucked away, a mock grill-work vent enabling them to hear every word.

One of those men, a king in an easy chair, was John Rooney, wearing a wrinkled, slightly shabby suit; more snappily dressed, in a chair at his left, sat his son, Connor, anxious but sober.

Nitti approached Rooney. "You heard?"

Rooney nodded. To his son, as if he couldn't stand the sight of him, he said, "Go upstairs."

Connor sat forward, urgent but rational. "Dad, listen to me. He's in the building—you can end this now!" After all, Nitti had more guns in this hotel than the Rock Island arsenal. "You've got to take him now."

The old man shook his head. "Connor—get upstairs."

Nitti almost smiled; how ridiculous it was, this grown man being sent to his room by his father! By all accounts, Connor was a fairly deadly character; he had been described to Nitti in varying ways, all unflattering: homicidal, unstable, volatile.

Yet the man wilted under his father's stare, and finally stalked out.

And when his son was gone, Rooney slumped in the chair, his head in his hands. "God help me. . . . What do I do?"

"You think objectively. And then you make your choice."

Nitti took the chair Connor had vacated. He had already told Rooney to cast emotion aside. To stay focused. To view this Sullivan as just another guy.

Rooney looked at Nitti with teary, rheumy eyes. "Make it quick."

Had to be quick . . . merciful. . . .

Nitti nodded. "Done . . . and the kid?"

Dismay exaggerated the old man's features. "Christ, no, no!" He'd already lost the wee one. . . .

Nitti had about had it up to here, from both Sullivan and Rooney, with this operatic crap. Right, fine, sure. "And then one day, the kid becomes a man. You think he won't remember?"

The old man considered that—Michael Sullivan, Jr., would surely never forget or forgive what Rooney's family had done to his family; still, he shook his head. "Not the kid."

"I understand," Nitti said, already mulling over who to get for an assignment this important, this hazardous. Someone freelance but trustworthy, someone worthy of the Angel of Death. . . .

"I know who to call," Nitti said, more to himself than Rooney. "He's done some jobs for us in the past—he's gifted. . . ."

9

Maguire was a yellow journalist—what was called a "picture chaser." He worked for big papers in several big cities, Milwaukee and Chicago among them, and when a photo was too gruesome even for the tabloid press, he peddled it to the even more exploitational newsstand crime magazines.

The gangland beat was his specialty—mob rubouts, in particular, though a good sex scandal or a celebrity autopsy also attracted his particular talent. His stature among the rags he worked for was based on his ability to show up at a grisly crime scene within moments of the carnage going down. He prowled the streets with a miniphoto lab in his trunk.

How Maguire became one of Frank Nitti's most reliable and fearsome hit men is unknown. But the assassin's research skills and—under the cover of his profession—his access as a legitimate reporter were invaluable. What else is a researcher but a hunter?

And Harlen Maguire was the perfect hunter.

* * *

Michael Sullivan, Sr., and his lovely wife, Annie.

John Rooney plays "grandpa" with Michael, Jr., and Peter.

Sullivan and Rooney tickle the ivories at Danny McGovern's wake.

John Rooney's unpredictable son, Connor.

John Rooney gets down to business.

Michael, Jr., goes about his paper delivery route.

Michael, Jr., learns the terrible truth about his father's profession.

The Angel of Death prays for the lives of those taken away.

Harlen Maguire captures another grisly scene of his own making.

Sullivan teaches his son the art of driving the getaway car.

The Angel of Death makes another call, this time on fastidious Mob accountant Alexander Rance.

Michael, Jr., anxiously awaits the return of his father.

Michael Sullivan comforts his son in one of their many hotel rooms.

The director of *Road to Perdition*, Sam Mendes.

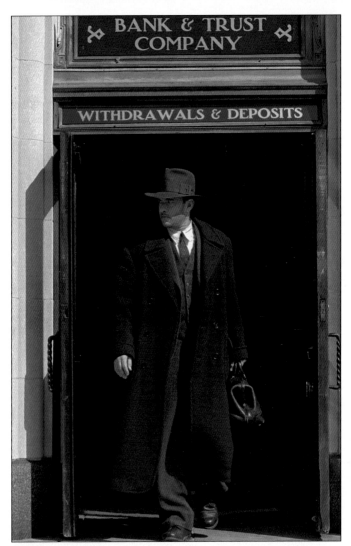

"Pray that God never puts you on my road. . . ."

The portable camera, with extendible tripod, weighed around forty pounds, but the slender man carrying it—pale, boyishly handsome, but nonetheless thirty years of age—moved quickly along the sidewalk, as if the apparatus he was hauling was featherlight.

Harlen Maguire might have been any reporter on the prowl for a good story, but the sharp cut of his suit, the rich fabric of his topcoat, and the snappy bowler said otherwise . . . though even a decent off-the-rack suit would have stood out in this neighborhood. This was Little Village, after all, a slum-ridden neighborhood on Chicago's West Side, where Italian blood often ran hot . . . and sometimes just ran.

Maguire figured the fire escape entrance to the tenement block would be less jammed, but a small crowd—undissuaded by the bitter winter morning chill—had gathered here as well. Most of them were out of work, and a juicy neighborhood murder was just the thing to warm the cockles.

Shouldering his way through, Maguire announced himself—"Press! Out of the way! Press! Excuse me, ma'am, thank you!"—and within a minute he was upstairs and inside the dingy one-room flat where, over by the kitchen area, police and a coroner's doctor were dealing with a man of average build in work shirt and denims who was slashed here and there, some nasty cuts that the guy didn't even seem to notice, ranting, raving about how he'd taken the knife away from some son of a bitch who had raped his wife.

No woman was present, so the cops had already gotten her out of there. And while they were dealing with the killer, Maguire would take a gander at the corpse.

His subject was in the bedroom corner of the flat, by a window looking out on the El tracks, a big oaf with his eyes and mouth open, sprawled on the floor with multiple stab wounds in his chest, like a bouquet of flowers: black entry gouges centered blossoms of red. His pants were embarrassingly down, his striped shorts discreetly up. The weapon was on the floor, a small hunting knife with blood smeared almost to the hilt.

Arms outstretched, there was a certain Pagliacci posture about the corpse that appealed to the photographer's sensibilities. This would be too much for the *Herald-American*, but the editor over at *Startling Detective* would pay through the nose—crimes of passion burned up the newsstands.

With swift precision Maguire assembled his tools, camera out of its case, tripod legs extending, bellows growing, and soon the artist was ready to go to work. To create something permanent out of the temporary, to make a sort of life out of death.

"Hey, could I have two minutes in here, please?"

He'd already slipped the cop—O'Ryan, who Maguire had run into on several prior occasions— a sawbuck.

"You got it, Mr. Maguire," O'Ryan said, and hauled himself out of there, the medic tagging after.

Then it was only the photographer and his subject, who was not likely to give him any problems. Maguire stepped behind the tripod and began to focus, the image of the corpse upside down in his viewfinder.

But just as he was about to take his shot, Maguire heard a bubbling cough . . . and he stepped from behind the camera and took a right-side-up look at the stiff.

Only this wasn't a stiff: the oaf was coughing, blood bubbling, trickling.

Maguire shook his head—son of a bitch was ruining everything. What was a crime of passion without a murder? He glanced at the closed door, and the rumble of an approaching train out on the El already was blotting out the pitiful groans of the uncooperative would-be corpse.

The photographer took a handkerchief from his pocket, then knelt over the victim; the man's open eyes had lost their blankness, consciousness glimmering in them now. So Maguire covered the man's bloody mouth with the hanky-in-hand, cupping it, squeezing the victim's nose closed.

As the El thundered past, the oaf struggled a little—not much, he'd have probably croaked on the way to the hospital, anyway—and Maguire looked into the man's eyes, watching the consciousness wink out, like the quenching of a candle.

Then the photographer wiped the fresh blood from the corpse's face, wadded up the handkerchief, slipped it in his pocket, and got back behind the tripod—with no more prima donna malarkey from his subject.

That same evening, Maguire was in his studio in his Chicago apartment. Bathed in the red glow of the darkroom, surrounded by shelves of his beloved cameras, he developed his photos. With tweezers, he fished a photo of the dead oaf out of the tray of fixing solution, then hung it up to dry. He was on photo number six, the last of the usable shots, when the phone rang.

With no sense of urgency, he wandered out into the living room of the small but nicely furnished flat, adorned with the artist's own work: framed photos of dead bodies, here a corpse in a pool hall, there a shot-up gangster in a corridor, here a bloody naked suicide in a bathtub. It was home to him—he just didn't bring his dates here.

Flopping on the sofa next to the phone on an end table, he answered with his usual, "Harlen Maguire."

"Frank Nitti," the assured voice said on the other end of the line.

Maguire scribbled on a pad as Nitti spoke, making notes, doodling, saying, "Un huh . . . Un huh," as the ganglord filled him in on the assignment, concluding, "This may take some time—some real tracking, some real research. What do you need?"

"Sixteen hundred dollars."

"That's more than last time."

"Sixteen hundred dollars is my rate, Mr. Nitti. And what I make on the photographs is mine."

"I'm not interested in photography, Mr. Maguire. But I do think creating evidence at the scene of your own crimes is reckless."

The gang boss then went into detail about the assignment. He needed Maguire to drop everything, to go right away. That was no problem, Maguire said. Nitti told him the funeral was tomorrow afternoon—a three-, maybe four-hour drive to the Tri-Cities. Maguire said he traveled light.

Nitti paused. "Did you ever run into this Sullivan character?"

"No, never met him. But I know his work."

"Angel of Death," Nitti said. "Pretty fancy moniker, well deserved."

Maguire knew all that already. "He traveling alone?"

Nitti's pause dripped with significance. "His son is with him."

"Uh-huh . . . how old?" A kid—that would be a first.

"Michael Sullivan, Jr.," Nitti was saying. "Twelve. Looks younger."

Maguire wrote the father's name plus the boy's name and age down, and then turned the 11 into a square and made it into a face, drawing hair, ears, and two dots for eyes.

"So," Maguire said, "what do I do with the kid?"

"What do you usually do with witnesses?"

"Un huh." He drew a down-turned mouth on the doodled face. "Will do."

And they said their good-byes, and he hung up, knowing he should have asked for more, for clipping the kid, but not wanting to cross Nitti. It wasn't a matter of being afraid of the gangster, though Nitti was not to be underestimated, former torpedo that he was. It wasn't that, at all. . . .

Maguire got up to straighten one of the framed photos—he'd noticed it hanging crooked as he spoke to Nitti. This shot was of a murder, or rather murders, he hadn't done; but one of his nicest compositions nonetheless: six corpses on the floor of S-M-C Cartage, brains spilling out of their shattered skulls—the seventh corpse had crawled out of frame, toward the door, compromising but not really spoiling this record of the St. Valentine's Day Massacre.

No, Maguire didn't want to risk losing the assignment.

He'd always wanted to meet the Angel of Death. And adding Michael Sullivan's portrait would be a crowning touch to his photo gallery.

As his father drove the rural off roads, Michael rode in the backseat so he could stretch out and nap or just rest, if he felt like it. But right now he was wide-awake, and he was glad when Papa—after a long interval of silence—struck up a conversation.

"Do you remember your aunt Sarah?"

Michael sat forward, leaned on the seat. "I think so."

"Your mom's sister, in Perdition. She'll take you in."

Still uncertain, the name of the town ringing no bell, Michael asked, "Where is it?"

"By the lake. We went there once, all of us, when you were four, maybe five." Papa looked over at him. "It's beautiful. . . . You remember?"

A memory was working its way to the surface. "The place with the dog?"

Papa glanced back at him, puzzled—not sure.

Michael explained about the place he remembered: this farm by a lake where they had a dog and it had jumped up at the table. "He ate Ma's sandwich that time."

Mama had given the whole sandwich to the pooch, saying once he'd had a bite, it was his.

His father glanced at him again, a tiny, tiny smile forming.

Michael could still remember their laughter, at the table; but he didn't feel like laughing now. Nor did Papa apparently. Because he was just staring at the road.

After a while, Michael asked his father why he'd mentioned the farm by the lake with Aunt Sarah and the dog.

"That's where we're going."

But that night they stayed in McGregor, Iowa, just another bump in the road with a town square and quiet streets. The Starr Motel was toward the edge

of the little farming community, a typical roadside
motor court. The room was clean but the furnishings
were old and cheap, the lighting dim and yellowish,
the covers and sheets worn, the kerosene space
heater smelly, and when the boy sat on the edge of
the bed and its thin mattress, the springs squeaked.

When they had traveled with Mama and Peter,
the family stayed in nicer places than this. Not that
he cared. The boy was preoccupied. He knew—he
just knew—that his father was going to dump him at
that place on some lake with this aunt who he barely
remembered.

The next day, when young Michael awoke, the
sun was filtering in brightly through the drawn curtains. An oily, metallic smell was in the air—like a
machine shop. He looked over toward his father's
bed and saw his father sitting there cross-legged like
an Indian, with newspapers spread out before him
on top of the covers and the parts of the tommy gun
arrayed like dishes of food on a picnic.

Papa had rags and various pipe-cleanerlike tools
and little bottles of stuff. He was methodically cleaning the pieces of the weapon. The pistol lay to one
side—either waiting its turn, or already finished
with.

The boy was shocked to find out it was two
o'clock in the afternoon. You were tired, his father
said; he'd slept a long time, too.

After Michael had washed up and gotten dressed,
they walked to the town square—it was only a few

blocks—and ate at a little café. Michael asked if he could have breakfast instead of lunch, and they were nice and fixed him eggs and bacon and pancakes. Papa ordered the blue plate special, which was meat loaf and mashed potatoes, but he didn't eat much of it.

Afterward, Papa said they were going to take a walk, and the day seemed cold and dreary for that, but Michael was in no position to argue. They crossed a little park and, a block off the business district, came to a small country church—a Catholic church. Michael quickly realized this was his father's destination—Papa must have spotted the church when they came into town.

In the gravel parking lot, Michael's father paused to explain what they were doing. There was a funeral today, he said. At this church? the boy wondered. No, back home, his father said, for Mama and Peter . . . and since Papa and Michael couldn't be there, they should go into this church and light candles for them, and pray.

Michael sat in a pew in the back of the church while his father knelt at the altar, praying before Christ on His cross. For a small church, they had a really big effigy of Christ—He looked real, and even from where Michael sat, the Lord's suffering was obvious. He watched as Papa lighted two candles—one for Mama, one for Peter.

Of the ninety-five acres of Chippiannock Cemetery, five were reserved for Catholic families. The Indians had called the place Manitou Ridge, and Sauk wives had raised corn on the fertile, gently sloping summit to feed the men encamped for war. The white people who turned it into a cemetery called it Chippiannock—an Indian word for "village of the dead."

A statue of a dog lay faithfully at the grave of a boy, five, and girl, three, who back in pioneer days had died of typhoid fever. An elaborate monument with a soldier on either side and an eagle atop cannon balls saluted the local fallen of American wars. Colonel George Davenport, the man for whom the city across the river was named, lay here on the Illinois side, not in Iowa. And stone cherubs and angels guarded the gray gravestones without complaint, underdressed though they were for the late-winter afternoon.

All of these made for good color, Maguire knew; he'd arrived an hour prior to the graveside services, and a sawbuck bought a nickel tour from a groundskeeper, with a few tidbits thrown in for free by a pair of gravediggers. The factual detective story magazines ate this stuff up almost as much as they did sex and slaughter.

As distant church bells tolled on cue, Maguire kept his distance at the back of the gathering of mourners—perhaps two dozen—attending the burial of Anne Louise Sullivan and Peter David Sullivan. There had been no church service, no mass. The circumstances were too strained, and strange, for that.

He didn't expect Sullivan to show—but you never knew. Some of these tough men had sentimental streaks a yard wide. So he kept watch, noting the armed bodyguards grouped around John Rooney, who was weeping, the goddamn hypocrite. No sign of his loony son Connor.

After the two flower-draped caskets were lowered, various mourners came up to a pleasant-looking, white-haired woman in her late forties, dressed in dignified black; they would introduce themselves and then express their condolences. This would be the surviving relative, clearly from out of town, to whom these sad arrangements and duties had fallen.

Dusk turned to evening as he followed several cars—including the funeral home limousine—to the house in Rock Island that matched the address Nitti had given him. The Sullivan family had lived in this fairly large two-story home—old Rooney had treated his top gunman well, up to the point where the guy's wife and kid got bumped off, anyway.

Cars pulled into the driveway, and drew up along the street in front, as various mourners paid their respects, going up to the door in little informal groups.

Maguire fell in with one of these mournful clusters, and slipped inside the home of the man—and boy—he was stalking.

With the bereaved relative occupied with her guests—food in the kitchen had been provided by neighbors—Maguire prowled the residence inconspicuously, taking in details like a hungry man took in a meal. He looked at old photos, family portraits of Annie and her kids together; Sullivan always seemed to stand to one side, vaguely detached.

Maguire understood that. Standing outside of yourself was necessary, when your profession was death. He had seen the same expression on the face of the mortician who'd been running the show at the graveyard this afternoon. And he had seen it in the mirror.

Some of the portraits had John Rooney in them—arms around the boys, at age four and five he'd guess . . . so very grandfatherly. How goddamn touching, Maguire thought. A middle-aged woman—Rooney's wife—was in some of the pictures, always standing next to the old man. She hadn't been at the services today. Dead, probably.

He asked where the bathroom was and someone pointed him upstairs. Glass of punch in hand, Maguire moved casually down the second-floor corridor; but once he was in the room that had been the boys' bedroom, he probed with surgical precision. In a drawer next to one of the boys' beds—the older boy?—he found a stash of Lone Ranger books. Beneath the mattress he discovered a pouch of Bugler tobacco . . . definitely the older boy, he thought with a smile.

In the master bedroom he found little of note, except perhaps the Catholic trappings—a crucifix, devotional paintings, Christ revealing His sacred heart. Tasteful, traditional nonsense. Maguire wondered if these beliefs were the dead wife's alone—if Sullivan had a religious streak, that might prove an Achilles' heel.

Sentimental—these killers could be so goddamn sentimental. Was Sullivan one of those clowns who thought he could put the killing in one compartment, and his family in another? That was a weak mental outlook—the fabled Angel of Death was just a man after all, a flawed man. . . .

Yet even as these thoughts flowed through his mind, Maguire knew he was trying to rationalize the intimidation he felt. He'd never had this big a challenge—and it was daunting.

And thrilling.

In the motel office, Sullivan handed the clerk a five spot and made the trunk call. Telling the operator the telephone number—that familiar number—gave Sullivan a twinge. He half expected Annie to answer, and the voice that did answer—"Hello, Sullivan residence"—had some of Annie in it.

Her sister, Sarah, and Annie were much alike, after all.

"Sarah?"

"Mike. Thank God. . . ."

"I want you to know we're okay."

"Where are you?"

"We're heading to your place, if that's all right."

Relief colored the voice. "Of course! I'll be back there in two days. . . . How's Michael?"

How could he answer that? "He's all right. . . . How was it?"

"Oh, Mike," Sarah said, too overcome to say any more.

She apparently thought he may have hung up, or the connection had been interrupted, and said, "Hello . . . ?"

"We'll see you soon," Sullivan said, tears spilling down his cheeks, and put the receiver in the hook.

And across the miles, in the house that had been Sullivan's, on the hallway phone that not long ago Connor Rooney had taken off the hook, the mourner who was actually Harlen Maguire quietly picked up the phone.

Once connected to the switchboard, he said, "Hello, operator? I was cut off—could you reconnect me?"

10

My memories of traveling with my father are something of a blur—when I think back, I see him behind the wheel, sometimes unshaven, sometimes not. When things between us were strained—as when I was pouting over him dragging me to Aunt Sarah's—I would ride in back, the whole seat to myself (me and the black tommy gun case, anyway), getting as far away from him as I could, in our little world that was the inside of the Ford.

My other memory is the heartland—middle America in all its vastness, sometimes rolling landscape, like a Grant Wood painting; other times flatness stretching to the horizon, winter barren, whites and browns and tans and grays. For every field there was a forest; for every ten barns, one church. The ribbons of concrete and gravel and dirt seemed to extend to eternity, endless sentences punctuated by the exclamation points of telephone poles—reminders that this pioneer country had been settled, that it was civilized now . . . even if I was sharing the backseat of a Ford with a Thompson submachine gun in a hard-shell case.

I can only speculate on what must have been going through Harlen Maguire's mind as he tracked us. Surely his photographer's eye had to have been struck by the abstract beauty of America's richest soil, masquerading in winter slumber as wasteland. Or was he too consumed with the mission at hand—was he focused hard on the empty road, a pistol and camera on the seat beside him?

Father and son were in Indiana now, traversing gently rolling farm country. They were cutting east across Highway 24, where at a town called Logansport they would take Highway 35 north, the road into Perdition, on Lake Michigan.

Sullivan stopped at a roadside diner outside tiny Wolcott, a boxcar whose WE NEVER CLOSE neon made a ghostly glow at dusk.

They had driven all day, Michael always in the backseat, and said little to each other. Sullivan was lost in thought, working out a plan to force Nitti and Capone to abandon their support of the Rooneys and turn Connor over to him. But he could not make it work, a man alone, and no matter how he mentally rearranged the cards, the hand he'd been dealt did not seem a winning one.

He knew his son was sulking, but that only made the boy less trouble, so he let it go. They'd eaten lunch at a smalltown café and the boy had again snookered the help into making him a breakfast. Sullivan's own appetite remained stunted, and he'd picked at his Salisbury steak.

Now, many hours of driving later, the man was

ready to give eating a try again; and his son should have some food.

In the boxcar diner's parking lot, Sullivan pulled into a stall adjacent to the window by an empty booth. He turned to his boy in the backseat. "You hungry?"

Michael didn't look at his father when he grunted, "No."

"Might not be another diner for a while," Sullivan said.

The boy shrugged.

"You should eat something."

"I'm not hungry. I wanna read."

That was all the effort Sullivan was prepared to give it, and he got out of the car, leaving the boy to his book and his brooding. Inside the brightly lit green-and-brown diner, business was slow for this close to suppertime—a farm couple in a booth having a meal, a farmer drinking coffee at the counter.

Leaving his topcoat and fedora on, he took the booth next to his car, where he could see Michael's head in the backseat, looking down at his book; he could also see the diner's door from here. A waitress came over, a blowsy brunette with plenty of lipstick and just as much personality. RUBY was stitched on her uniform blouse. She brought water and coffee.

Hunger was finally stirring, and Sullivan also thought he might be able to stir his son into eating by making a show of a meal. So he ordered a T-bone, rare.

He'd been waiting for the food maybe five minutes when the bell over the door dinged, and just as
the farm couple was leaving, a cop came in—a man
in his forties who'd never missed a meal. The blue
uniform indicated a town cop, not a sheriff's man or
state policeman.

The cop settled on a stool near, but not next to, the
farmer who was having a piece of apple pie.

Sullivan considered leaving, but Ruby was on her
way with his steak, smelling very good indeed (the
steak—Ruby's perfume was another matter), and his
instincts said the cop's presence was innocent. So he
sat in the booth and dug in, using a steak knife on
the nice piece of cornfed Midwestern beef. He
glanced out the window to see if this was tempting
Michael, but the boy's head was no longer visible.

Knowing the boy was probably stretched out
sleeping, Sullivan nonetheless wondered if he
should go out there and check on him. Night had
smothered dusk, and that was just enough to make
Sullivan edgy. He was sipping his coffee, looking out
the window at the Michael-less backseat window
when the bright sweep of headlights, a vehicle coming into the diner parking lot, made him wince.

The driver parked, got out—Sullivan noted the
uptown topcoat and bowler as atypical for this rural
area—and glanced at the cop car in the lot. Something about the glance was less casual than it tried to
be. In his booth by the window, Sullivan craned his
neck, trying to see the front license plate, couldn't,

and as the bell over the door dinged, he returned to his meal.

Sullivan seemed to be looking at nothing in particular, but he noted the way the newcomer was registering the farmer at the counter . . . and especially the cop. Right now Sullivan was the only other patron. Dark-haired but pale, the guy had a narrow, angular face—youthful, though Sullivan made him as around thirty.

The man took the booth next to Sullivan's, but sat opposite him, the two men facing each other—and right now both were going out of their way not to look at each other.

Water and coffee in hand, Ruby approached the new customer, who said to her, "Slow night, huh?"

"You kiddin'? This is busy! What can I get you?"

"You got a special?"

"Honey, everything's special."

"Is that so?"

"Everything 'cept the food."

The guy laughed at that—giving the remark a little more reaction than it deserved. "'Everything 'cept the food!' Ruby, you oughta be on the stage."

"Don't I know it."

Still chuckling, glancing at the menu, the man said, "Gimme some of that honey-dip fried chicken, and a black coffee."

"Duck soup," the cheerful waitress said, and sauntered off.

The customer reached into his topcoat pocket and withdrew a camera and a roll of film. He began to load the camera, Sullivan noting all this, without seeming to.

Reaching in his own topcoat pocket, Sullivan got out his small silver flask. Putting a little weave into his actions, he poured whiskey into his coffee cup.

"Don't mind me, sir," the man said.

Sullivan glanced up, seemingly unsteady, and—putting a tiny slur in his voice, not overdoing it—replied, "Huh?"

The man leaned forward and whispered, as if keeping this conversation from the cop at the counter. "It's a free country—used to be, anyhow."

Eyes half-hooded, Sullivan smiled, poured more whiskey into the cup, hoping he was playing his role more convincingly than the fellow in the next booth was. Too friendly, way too friendly. . . .

Sullivan raised the flask, in offering.

The man raised a hand. "No, thank you, sir." Then he returned to loading the camera, snapping it shut, fully loaded now.

"Your profession?" Sullivan asked, voice wavering slightly, referring to the camera. "Or your pleasure?"

"Both, I guess," the guy said with a shrug. He had cold eyes that didn't blink much; he'd probably worn that same smile, Sullivan thought, when he was a kid pulling the wings off flies.

"To be paid to do," the man was saying, "what you love . . . ain't that the American dream?"

Sullivan lifted his shoulders, set them down, as if

the action required both thought and effort. "Guess so."

"Yourself?"

Sullivan blinked, thinking that over. "I'm *in* business."

"I knew it!" the guy said. "When I saw that fancy automobile, I thought, 'There sits a businessman.'"

Sullivan twitched a smile.

"What's your business?"

"Salesman. Machine parts."

"Machine parts. That's wonderful!" He babbled about the wheels that make the world go round— such vital work.

"I assure you," Sullivan said, "it is not. So—who do *you* work for?"

Eyebrows lifted. "Can you keep a secret?" He sat forward again, whispering, "I'm 'press' . . ."

Sullivan pretended to be impressed. "Which paper?"

"All over. I'm something of a rarity," the guy claimed.

"How's that?"

He grinned wickedly. "I shoot the dead."

Sullivan tilted his head—what say?

"Dead bodies, that is." He held up his hands in mock surrender, made a comic face. "*I* don't kill 'em!"

With a laugh, Sullivan said, "Should hope not."

Crime scenes, the guy explained—the grislier the better—that's what pleased his bloodthirsty editors.

Ruby came over to see if Sullivan needed more

coffee. He said he didn't. She asked if he wanted a slice of pie. He said no. Then she refilled the photographer's cup and went back behind the counter.

The photographer picked up where he'd left off: "Always fascinated me—the look of 'em!"

A corpse, he meant.

Sullivan shivered—he was trying to keep a meal down.

But his new friend reminded him that the world needed people who aren't afraid to look at unpleasantness. Where would society be without doctors? Without morticians?

Sullivan shrugged.

The look of a person, right after life has left him, was so intriguing. "Ever see one?" he asked Sullivan, meaning a dead body. He didn't mean in a coffin . . . but within minutes, seconds, of their last breath.

Sullivan nodded.

"Sorry for you," the guy said unconvincingly. "Terrible thing . . ." And now an inappropriate grin. "But it sure makes you feel alive, don't it?"

Sullivan raised his coffee cup. "I'll drink to that."

The man was eyeing the cop at the counter, who was finishing up, paying Ruby.

Then those unblinking eyes narrowed as they fixed themselves again on Sullivan. "Stuff makes you sweat, huh?"

Sullivan nodded. "Piss, too," he said, surreptitiously slipping a butter knife off the table. He scooched out of the booth. "Excuse, ma'am, where's the bathroom?"

Once told, he began to make his way to the john, stumbling as he went.

Harlen Maguire turned around in the booth, wondering if Mike Sullivan was as drunk as he seemed. Half a minute passed, and the bell over the door dinged—the cop going out.

Maguire reached in his jacket pocket, withdrew the .38 revolver, keeping it out of sight beneath the counter. A car started up, pulled out. Good. With the cop gone, Maguire had no problem with what lay ahead of him—a farmer, a waitress, a cook. The gleaming tile of the diner, with its chrome fixtures splashed with blood (red registering black on film), littered with corpses . . . what a picture. He wouldn't even need a flash.

The bell over the door dinged—okay, one more customer, just another element of his composition—*but it was the cop again!*

Ambling in, the officer came over to Ruby, grinning embarrassedly. "Forgot to leave a tip!"

And Maguire flew out of the booth, out of the diner, and the Ford was gone—he could hear it accelerating down the highway, roaring off.

Shit!

He ran to his own car—the Illinois plates screaming at him: *Idiot!*—and found his tires slashed . . . four goddamn flats!

Cop inside or not, Maguire ran into the road where Sullivan's taillights receded into the distance, and slowly, steadily, he aimed the long-barreled revolver.

In the Ford, Sullivan—not drunk, though rolling down the window one-handed, to combat the whiskey he'd chugged for the sake of show—was yelling at his boy: "Get down!"

Michael, waking up in the backseat, popped his head up, saying, *"Why? What's goin' on—"*

"Get down!"

And his father reached back and physically shoved him down as the rear window exploded.

Behind them, pleased at the sound of the shattered glass, Maguire fired again, this time with no success.

Damnit, he thought, standing in the road.

The cop, having heard the shot, came running out, one hand unbuttoning a holstered sidearm. "Hey! What do you think you're doing—"

Maguire turned and shot him. Twice.

Blood mist blossomed in the night as the dead cop tumbled onto his back. With a sigh, Maguire took his gun and his camera and headed back into the diner to finish up.

Sullivan drove the speed limit, relieved that no headlights were coming up behind him, grateful for the dark night and the empty highway. He was heading across Highway 24, back toward where they'd come, the turnoff to the Perdition road no longer an option.

In his cap and heavy winter coat, pushed down

by his papa, Michael hadn't been hurt by the flying glass—neither had Sullivan—and shards lay in the backseat like scattered ice.

As the boy sat in stunned silence, Sullivan took a side road. A few miles later, he drove up into the entry of an open field and after perhaps a half mile stopped the car, cutting the lights. The man with the camera would not find them here.

Out of breath, he turned to his son, who was wide-eyed and also breathing hard. Fury rose in Sullivan like lava, erupting: "When I say get down, you get down! You don't ask questions."

There was no time for questions. You could die in the time it took to ask a question!

"If I say we're stopping to eat, you stay with me!"

The boy started to protest, but his father's voice rolled over him.

"You listen to what I say from now on, or you can get out of the car and take care of yourself."

The boy's eyes were huge.

"Make up your mind, Michael! I can't fight them and you at the same time."

And now the boy got mad, shouting defensively, "I can take care of myself fine! You think it's my fault this happened! You never wanted me along anyway."

"Stop it, Michael! It was not your fault—none of it."

This seemed to register on the boy; but he still sounded angry when he said, "Just take me to Aunt Sarah's."

He shook his head. "I can't take you there—not now."

"Why?"

"*He* knows that's where we're going."

The boy said, "So . . . what are we going to do?"

"Something I can't do alone."

The man had been thinking about doing something . . . but he hadn't been able to figure out a way to do it on his own. With Michael helping, he could make it work. But it would be dangerous.

The boy didn't care. He just wanted to be with his father; he just wanted to help.

He held his son's eyes with his. "Then you have to *listen* to me now. Okay? Or we'll both be dead."

Michael nodded.

"I have to make Capone give up Connor. . . ."

The boy nodded again, following.

"Now," Sullivan continued, "there's one thing more important to Chicago than anything—and that's their money."

These men in Chicago, they talked about loyalty and honor and family, Sullivan told his son, but what they really cared about was money.

And these big men, Capone and Nitti, kept their money in little banks around the Midwest. Sort of . . . spread around, for safety sake. These were the same ones the boy's godfather used . . . hiding money from the government, for tax reasons. And Sullivan knew where these banks Chicago used were.

"They keep it in banks all over," Sullivan told the

boy, meaning Capone's money. "What we have to do is find it . . . and take it."

Michael's eyes got big again.

"Are you going to help me?" Sullivan asked his son.

"Yes," the boy said.

No hesitation.

"Then," Sullivan said, "I'm going to teach you something."

How to be a wheelman.

And when Michael said he didn't know what a wheelman was, Sullivan promised him that first thing tomorrow, after breakfast, the boy would see.

11

For my father and me, the road to Perdition was ever-winding and (or so it seemed to me then) never-ending. We could have been to the farm by the lake a thousand times in those long weeks. We traversed the same Midwestern states often enough—dirt roads, gravel roads, occasionally concrete, ever traveling, ever nearing, never arriving.

So in a way, the real start of our journey began the morning after that man with the camera tried to kill us at the diner.

And on that morning—when I had my first lesson as my father's underage wheelman—I accomplished something that all of Capone's thugs (and Rooney's, too) never could: I frightened my father. Not that my father was immune to fear, and I don't mean to suggest that the various scrapes and shoot-outs with gangsters and assassins didn't affect him.

But no gangster, however hard-boiled, however ruthless, managed to do what I did—turn my father's face white.

*   *   *

The next morning—while a service station re-
paired the Ford's rear window—Michael's father
gathered some items at the motel, and they had a
nice breakfast at another diner, where, between bites
of toast and nibbles of crisp bacon, Papa gave
Michael the first part of the driving lesson. He told
the boy about the gears and the clutch and the brake,
and the boy—so excited he could barely eat—
grinned and nodded and took it all in . . . or anyway
thought he had.

Before long they were on the road again, Papa behind the wheel in his dark topcoat and fedora, looking serene, even comfortable as he turned off the
main highway onto a farm road, where right now
they seemed to be the only traffic. Soon he pulled
over and got out, telling the boy to do the same.

From the compartment under the backseat Papa
collected the items he'd rounded up at the motel—a
stack of newspapers he piled on the seat behind the
wheel, and pieces of blocklike wood that he tied
with twine to the various pedals. His father didn't
explain, but Michael realized this was to enable him
to sit higher and reach those pedals easier.

This took quite a while, and by the time Papa had
finished, Michael's heart was a triphammer—he
wasn't scared, not really . . . more exhilarated and
even astonished. How many fathers would entrust
their car to a boy his age? Who needed a bicycle,
anyway? Kid's stuff.

Michael turned the key in the ignition and it

seemed wondrous, the way the engine burst to thrumming life. How many times had he sat in this car with his father and mother and taken that magic for granted.

Michael turned to his father, who remained casual, composed, the car throbbing.

"Now you know what the clutch is?"

"Sure I know what the clutch is!"

"What's the clutch?"

The boy shrugged. "The clutch . . . it"—he gestured, tried again—"the clutch . . . it . . . it . . . clutches."

"Right. It clutches. And which of those pedals does the clutching?"

Michael put his foot on one of the blocks-tied-to-pedals and pressed. The engine roared, and he reared back from the wheel.

"That's the gas," his father said. The accelerator, he explained.

And the boy blinked and said, sure—it accelerates.

His father nodded. "Let me show you the clutch."

Then the car was moving forward, a few feet, and Michael tried to put it in gear; but the car shuddered to a stop.

"Let's go again." His father reached over, started the car again, and Michael looked at him, asking, "Release gas, clutch, shift gear, hit gas?"

"Mmm-hmm."

Michael tried that sequence—and the car lurched forward!

Amazed, pleased, Michael cried, "And shift!"

The car stopped—died again.

They sat in exasperated silence for a moment; then his father asked, gently, "May I make one suggestion?"

"No! I'm doing this."

His father's eyebrows raised, but the boy didn't sense the man's amusement.

Before long, however, Michael was driving, the car crawling along the country road . . . but moving.

"Good," Sullivan told his son. "Now—I'm going to need you to go a little faster."

"Right now?"

Sullivan explained that when he came out of a bank with the bank's money, he didn't want the police to be able to catch them by running alongside the car. The mention of police widened the boy's eyes.

He calmed his son with a look, and said, "It's a good idea to practice."

The boy nodded—faster, then . . .

And before long Michael wasn't just driving . . . he was really driving—zooming! But the boy was steering the wheel like in the moving pictures, like a cartoon bug driving a cartoon car, and his father settled him down, and then the car moved straight and steady . . . and fast.

Farmland seemed to whiz by on either side of them.

"Michael, easy."

But the boy was having a great time, unaware how barely in control of the vehicle he was.

"Easy, Michael! Forty-five miles an hour is too fast."

Suddenly, as if it materialized, a tractor was up ahead of them, moving very slowly.

"Michael, watch out for the tractor."

Had this been a field, the tractor would have been doing fine, clipping right along—but on a road, the machine beast was crawling, and the boy was stunned by how fast they had come up on it. . . .

"*Watch out for the—*" His father seemed to be trying to climb through the windshield. "*Son of a bitch!*"

Instinctively, the boy whipped around the tractor, shrieking past, and when he glanced over, his father was white, his eyes wide . . . afraid, really really afraid.

"We made it!" Michael said, excited, relieved, elated.

"Yeah, yeah, we made it," his father said dryly, settling back into his seat, color climbing back into his face.

They had a few more close calls, and when a hay wagon crossed the road ahead of them, the boy hit what he hoped was the right pedal and the Ford squealed to a stop, thrusting son and father forward.

Michael, loving this, told his father he thought these brakes were swell; then he asked Papa if he was all right . . . The man looked a little sick.

But Papa said that he was fine, and that Michael was doing fine, too. He noted that it looked hilly, a few miles up ahead, and said this would be a good time to practice taking curves.

Other than the scrape with the tractor, Papa never raised his voice once. He stayed at it, working with his son, guiding him, giving him confidence; and by midafternoon, they were in St. Louis, Missouri, where the boy—sitting high enough in his seat to pass for a teenaged driver—got his first taste of sharing the road with other drivers, not all of them considerate. This came easier than his father had expected—but ex-paperboy Michael had, after all, maneuvered his bike through all kinds of traffic back home.

And by the end of the day, Michael Sullivan, Jr., was ready for his new job.

The next morning, Sullivan—his fedora and topcoat brushed, his dark suit, too—approached the entrance of a bank and trust company. With his no-nonsense manner, a black leather bag in his right hand, he looked better than just presentable—he might have been a doctor, or perhaps a businessman, lugging a valise filled with important papers.

The boy waited down the street, in a legal parking place, motor running. Sullivan nodded at his son, who, behind the wheel, swallowed and nodded back.

The high-ceilinged marble lobby was less than crowded, but a share of farmers, housewives, and businessmen stood at the teller windows in lines that weren't moving fast. He paused inside the door, nodding to a bank guard, who nodded back—an older man, retired cop probably, but armed.

Heading across the lobby at a leisurely pace, Sullivan gave the place a slow scan, mentally recording the layout, the positions of people and things. He approached the teller windows, heading toward one that was closed, where a small browbeaten man in glasses and bow tie and shirtsleeves was getting chewed out by an older, heavier man, also in glasses, but wearing a crisply knotted striped tie and a tailored suit amid these off-the-racks.

Sullivan waited until the officious man seemed finished, then said through the window grating, "Excuse me—I'm looking for a Mr. McDougal."

But apparently the officious man wasn't quite through yet, and he raised a finger to Sullivan, in a "one moment" manner, saying to the clerk, "You ask for proper identification or you'll find yourself without employment."

The clerk nodded and mumbled a dutiful response.

Then the man in charge turned to Sullivan and said, with no more respect than he'd shown his employee, "Yes, sir—how may I help you?"

It turned out the officious man was the manager of the bank, Mr. McDougal himself, who informed Sullivan that he would have to make an appointment with his secretary.

Then Sullivan apologized for not calling ahead, but he informed McDougal that this visit concerned a major depositor—from out of town. The banker again began to speak, but the words caught as he took a closer look at Sullivan.

McDougal led the way, even opened the door for Sullivan with an after-you half bow, closing the door behind him, making a fuss over showing his visitor to the chair across from the big desk in the medium-sized office dominated by a huge safe. Officiousness had been replaced with obsequiousness as the bank manager took the chair behind the desk, eyeing the black bag Sullivan had placed on its glass-covered top, off to one side, by framed photos of wife, grown children, and grandchildren.

"I've come in regards to the Chicago money you're holding," Sullivan said.

"Well, this is a pleasant surprise," the bank manager said, hands folded like a man sitting down to a big fine meal. "I wasn't expecting a deposit until the end of the month."

"Actually," Sullivan said, reaching over for the bag and undoing its clasp, "I'm making a withdrawal."

And Sullivan dipped down into the bag and came back with the Colt .45.

McDougal's ass-kissing smile disappeared—fear painted the man's face a pale shade.

Sullivan told him to keep his hands on the desk and listen carefully. "I want dirty money only. Everything that you're holding for Capone that's off-the-books. . . . Open the safe."

The terrified banker turned around to the safe behind his desk and dialed the combination—it took several tries, nervous as he was; but soon McDougal was hauling out a safe-deposit box, which he rested on the desk, opening it to reveal stacks and stacks of cash.

During this procedure, Sullivan said, "And if I read anything about this in the papers . . . if I read that the savings of innocent farmers were wiped out by a heartless bank robber . . . I'll be unhappy."

McDougal swallowed, nodded.

"Open the box," Sullivan said.

As he piled the bricks of cash into the bag, the banker—still nervous but past the shock, somewhat—said, "You're insane. You know they'll find out who you are. . . ."

"The name is Sullivan. . . . Want me to spell it?"

Sullivan took the bag of money from the banker—who was more astounded now than afraid.

"They'll kill you," the banker said, trying to fathom this event. "They're animals."

"You don't say. Put it in."

Sullivan stopped the banker from placing the last two fat wads of cash from the satchel. "This is for you. Call it a handling charge. . . . Tell Chicago I took it."

Sullivan nodded as the banker pocketed the cash.

The banker was shaking his head again. "You really trust me not to say anything?"

"Always trust a bank manager," Sullivan said, hoisting the satchel of money, touching the tip of his fedora.

Within a minute Sullivan—black bag in one hand, other hand with the gun in it shoved into his topcoat pocket—was standing outside the bank, stepping out to the curb, waiting in the chill St. Louis air. And within seconds, the Ford drew up slowly.

Sullivan looked through the window at the anxious boy behind the wheel.

"No rush," he said to his son.

He got in, and they drove off.

12

Over the next two weeks, my father and I knocked over four banks, and that was just the beginning. At the time I wondered why we put so many days between robberies; looking back, I realize my father was craftily creating a nonpattern, a patchwork of plunder that defied analysis. It made for a lot of driving, but a bank in Illinois would be followed by one in Nebraska; Iowa might be followed by Oklahoma, with him filling his satchel in Wisconsin next.

We could certainly afford the gas.

The compartment in the backseat, where I had hidden myself away on that rainy night, was stacked with bricks of money, decorated with various bank wrappers. And we were probably on the fourth robbery before my father finally explained the absence of gunfire and police.

His pattern was always the same—politely announcing himself as a representative of Chicago, revealing his gun in the bank president's office, the gathering of the money, a sharing of the proceeds with the banker, and a threatening but almost courteous exit. After the first several of the robberies, the word had spread and most of the bankers seemed to be waiting for my father—in a good way . . . eager for their bonus.

It was a good thing, too, that these holdups were so nonviolent, because I didn't get the hang of my wheelman role all at once. The lack of a parking place on our second job sent me around the block, and I got turned around somehow, and left my father cooling his heels at the curb with a bag of money in one hand and a gun in the other (in his topcoat pocket). He probably stood there less than a minute, but it must have seemed a lifetime before I showed up—coming in the wrong direction, hitting the curb, making Papa jump back.

But every time I got better, and I was probably as smooth and professional a getaway driver as anybody in the outlaw game—Bonnie and Clyde, and Ma Barker and her boys, had nothing on the Sullivans.

It didn't take long for the Chicago forces to get wise to our tactics—not the aiding and abetting of the bankers, but that Michael Sullivan was plundering their hidden coffers. After all, Papa advertised it—encouraged the bankers who were in collusion with him to tell Chicago the looting would stop only when Connor was turned over to him.

So after the fourth robbery, we found a farmhouse where the people were away, and borrowed their barn to turn our Ford maroon. Good thing, too, because on the fifth robbery, we rolled up to find a contingent of thugs milling around outside the bank Papa had chosen.

My father nodded at me, and I drove away. No problem. The Capone money was spread around in too many

*banks all over the Midwest for goon squads to be sent to
all of them.*

They had robbed their fifth bank—in Loose
Creek, Missouri—that morning; it was evening and
the father and son were in an informal supper club
in Farmington, Iowa. The place had a homey feel—a
few booths, more tables, picnic-style tablecloths, curtains on the windows, the light soft and warm and
yellow.   •

Sullivan and his son sat at a small table near an
improvised dance floor, where a couple of couples
danced to the radio—right now that new jazz singer,
Bing Crosby, was singing "Where the Blue of the
Night Meets the Gold of the Day." The singer's warm
voice, his casual style, pleased Sullivan. Both he and
his boy were having the meat loaf with mashed potatoes and creamed corn; both ate heartily.

Their waitress—whose name, BETTY, was stitched
on her neck-high apron—came over to see how they
were doing. She was probably forty, a slender
brunette with dark red lipstick, though not heavily
made-up. A nice girl. Nice woman.

"Coffee?" she asked.

"Thanks," Sullivan said.

She noticed him looking her over, and their eyes
met, and hers told his she didn't mind the friendly
once-over.

"So . . . what brings you guys to the middle of
nowhere?" she asked.

Michael, turning a piece of white bread brown by

mopping up gravy, said brightly, "We're bank robbers!"

His father gave him a look, but Betty just laughed.

"We're just passing through," Sullivan said.

She accepted this noninformation with a smile, and he watched as she headed behind the counter, taking off her apron. The restaurant was about to close.

His plate clean, Michael pushed it forward and, as if inquiring about dessert, asked, "So—when do I get my share of the money?"

Sullivan thought about that. "How much d'you want?"

The boy clearly hadn't expected such an open-ended response, and Sullivan watched with amusement as his son's face registered the effort to come up with a suitably high, but not outrageous, figure.

"Two hundred dollars," the boy said firmly.

"Okay. Deal," Sullivan said.

Michael frowned. "Could I have had more?"

Sullivan sipped his coffee. "You'll never know."

One of the dancers went over to the console radio and turned it up, not long before Crosby came to his big finish, the music swelling.

In the executive suite on the top floor of the Hotel Lexington in Chicago, Frank Nitti—impeccable in a gray pin-striped suit, immaculately groomed right down to every hair on his mustache—listened on the phone as Harlen Maguire gave him the latest bad news.

Then he exploded into the phone: "How much did he take? *How* much?"

The voice on the end of the wire said, "Seventy-five thousand, Mr. Nitti—everything you had with them. . . . He told the bank president he'd kill him, otherwise."

Maguire went on to say that Sullivan had again given the banker his name, and the former Rooney enforcer had said that he was prepared to give up his "fun," as he called it, if the Capone Outfit turned over Connor Rooney to him.

"So," Nitti calmly said to Maguire into the phone, "answer me this."

"Certainly."

Nitti spat the words: *"What are we paying you for?"*

Maguire was making excuses in the ganglord's ear as the door burst open and Connor Rooney stalked in, the bodyguard Nitti had assigned to him, Little Louis Campagna, on the man's heels. Rooney was not drunk at least, but he looked terrible, his suit rumpled, his complexion gray and waxy—like he hadn't slept in days. Weeks.

"What?" Nitti snapped at his uninvited guest. "What . . . what the fuck is this?" He had made it clear to the younger Rooney that just because the man was staying at the Lexington didn't mean he didn't have to make an appointment like anybody else. Nitti was working!

"Where's my father?" Connor demanded, standing right across from Nitti.

Nitti flinched a nonsmile.

Connor raved on. He had been calling the Twentieth Street mansion in Rock Island—and his father's office, too—trying everywhere. He was either not there (whoever answered would say), or there would be no answer.

Nitti shrugged.

The slender gangster began to pace. Campagna took a step back, but kept an eye on his charge. Connor was still ranting—had his own father turned his back on him? "Why is no one talking to me?" he wanted to know. "I feel like a fucking prisoner!"

Nitti, arms folded, composed in the detached way he preferred, said, "You're not a prisoner, Connor. You're being protected.... This is what your father wants."

Connor came back over to the desk, leaned on it, his expression indignant, eyes flaring. "I can look after myself."

"No," Nitti said. "You can't. This is the point: you're a big baby who doesn't know his thumb from his own dick."

Connor's eyes flared again, nostrils too, like a rearing horse. "Fuck you!"

Nitti was cool, calm, as he replied: "Listen, sonny . . . the only thing keeping you alive is being John Rooney's son. Your father covered Capone's back more than once . . . and Al doesn't forget."

Connor planted himself in front of the desk now. "You're being a little shortsighted, Frank. . . . My father's an old man. What you're *protecting* is your future." He gestured to himself with a hitchhiker thumb. "*I'm* the future."

Nitti said nothing. He didn't have to be told what a gold mine the Tri-Cities area was . . . or that Rooney was an old man. Or for that matter that Connor Rooney was a lunatic.

Still, Connor seemed intent on making that very point, raving, "So don't you *ever* talk to me that way again." His upper lip curled back over his teeth.

Connor stormed off.

Nitti sighed and picked up the phone again. "Maguire? You still there?"

"Yes . . . I heard most of that."

"Look, do what you have to do. . . . *Find them.*"

"I'm taking steps," Maguire said.

Nitti told his man that steps didn't make it—he should try leaps; but Maguire pointed out that Sullivan was hopping around a three-state area.

Impatient, Nitti said again, "Just do what you have to do."

And he doubled the photographer's retainer.

Maguire thanked Nitti for his generosity, and the ganglord told the photographer to wait to see how generous Frank Nitti would be on the day Maguire found Sullivan and his son.

"I'll do what I can, Mr. Nitti," Maguire said. "But I think this might take some time. . . ."

13

As the weeks rolled by, my father filled his black satchel at banks in Iowa and Illinois, Nebraska and Oklahoma, Missouri and Kansas, even Indiana and Wisconsin. Never was a shot fired, and our holdups became as close to routine as bank robbery could get.

Sometimes at night, when my father grew tired behind the wheel, we would sleep in the car. I disliked this, and most of the time he tried to find motels, or at least campsites where, when we parked, a few of the amenities of civilization were on hand.

As we traveled, Papa would read the papers religiously, looking for mention of our robberies, never finding anything, and that pleased him. He was less happy about the lack of other news. He never said, but upon reflection, I understand he was thumbing through the pages of papers looking for a mention of Connor Rooney's body turning up in a ditch somewhere, signaling Chicago's surrender and an end for our journey.

*　　*　　*

At the Grand Prairie State Bank in Grand Prairie, Oklahoma, Mike Sullivan was sitting across the desk from a bank manager, a younger man than most in his position. Very professional in dress and manner, the young bank manager was nervous, and clearly frightened.

"I'm sorry, Mr. Sullivan." The bank manager, his eyes wide, shrugged helplessly. "There's no money."

The gun snapped into position, leveled directly at the bank manager's head.

"No! No . . . I can get you *money*," the man said. "I just . . . It won't be Chicago's. They took it all out two days ago."

Sullivan had been studying the man; the truth was written on his smooth young face.

"Who authorized it?"

"The accountant."

A mob accountant from Chicago had been going around, it seemed, accompanied by armed men, to all the banks. He'd been doing it for days, the bank manager said.

"What was his name?" Sullivan asked, knowing.

"Rance," the bank manager said. "Alexander Rance."

Alexander Rance—the mob accountant Joe Kelly had brought to the Rooney board meeting, to try to make the case for getting involved with the unions.

Sullivan asked, "You wouldn't happen to know what Mr. Rance's next stop is, would you?"

"Actually, I do."

14

Alexander Rance represented Frank Nitti's shift toward a big business stance, including moving into legitimate enterprises.

The smooth Rance was like so many accountants and lawyers in that small white-collar army who did the bidding of thugs-made-good like Frank Nitti. A fussy man, particular about his food, dress, and lodging, Rance operated on Outfit finances in a fashion that isolated him from the violence inherent in such criminal activities as gambling, loan-sharking, prostitution, and bootlegging.

The accountant probably had no idea how much danger he was in when Nitti directed him to personally supervise the removal of mob money from Midwestern banks. Rance was to select a hotel from which he could operate, in a given area, withdraw the money, and send it home to Chicago under armed guard, where the funds would go into safe-deposit boxes in the kind of large, reputable Chicago banks that would be unlikely targets for my father.

Rance would seek a luxury hotel in a smaller town. He

would then check into the bridal suite, apparently because that would represent the nicest accommodations available, and take all of his meals via room service, asking to speak to the chef, to whom he gave copious instructions on the preparation of his meals.

Breakfast in particular was a ritual to Rance—boiled eggs, runny, with crisp bacon . . . but not so crisp that the strips would break off when he inserted them into the yolk.

When father and son pulled into Stillwater, Oklahoma, the wear and grime of the road showed on them. They were a grubby, hardened-looking pair, the boy behind the wheel of the maroon Ford well aware that his father was possessed by a quiet apprehension that seemed a notch up from recent days.

On a gentle slope of Stillwater Creek, the idyllic small town spread northwest; large, comfortable-looking residences sat in big yards half hidden by trees, and the business district consisted of low, trim buildings. The relative grandeur of the aptly named Grand Hotel belied the town's modest appearance, and gave away its secret: this was a center of business and agriculture, within easy driving distance of most Oklahomans.

Pulling into the spot like the seasoned driver he now was, the boy asked, "Pa—can we stay at a motel tonight? I hate sleeping in the car."

"All right, that would be nice," Sullivan said, checking the clip in the automatic. He had an extra clip in his topcoat pocket. Going into unknown territory like this, such preparations were key. He slapped the ammo into the .45. "Now if you see any-thing, you hit the horn two times."

The boy nodded.

"And don't get out of the car."

Sullivan leaned close to the boy, locked eyes with him, and reminded Michael that he might hear shots, screams, or nothing at all—whatever the case, he was not to leave the Ford.

"No matter what," Sullivan insisted.

Again the boy nodded.

"Okay," Sullivan said. "You ready?"

The boy took a deep breath. "I'm ready."

Sullivan told the boy to stay alert, and got out of the car.

From where they had parked, the boy watched in the driver's-side-door mirror as his father strode confidently, yet casually, into the fancy hotel.

In a dreary, functionally furnished apartment above a storefront across from the Grand Hotel, Betty Lou Petersen was sitting on the edge of the bed, pulling on her silk stockings.

Otherwise, the curly-haired blonde teenager was fully dressed, the first time in the two days since she had hooked up at the Stillwater Tap with the man who stood opposite her, his back to her, in his T-shirt and shorts, at a window looking down into the main street.

A year ago Betty Lou had been a cheerleader at Stillwater High School; now she was an unwed mother and one of the town's youngest, most attractive prostitutes, although she had not yet admitted that to herself, thinking she was just a party girl who took favors from men. Betty Lou lived at home with her widowed mama, who looked after little Violet when Betty Lou was out "having a good time."

The man in his underwear at the window was a handsome date, but an odd one. His clothes (when he was wearing them) were uptown, and he had good manners; he smelled like pomade and talcum and was very, very clean. Also, he was fairly young and nicely slender, not like some of the traveling salesmen and businessmen she entertained, who had flabby bellies and body odor.

Still, she wasn't sorry this party was over. A few minutes ago, he'd ignored her, when she asked him, "How many more days you gonna want me, mister?"

Nothing.

She tried again, saying, "Can't we close the curtains even for a little while? I can't get no sleep with all that light."

Finally he threw some money on the bed and said, "Good-bye." That word, and the two crumpled twenties, were all she got out of him, except for the cold shoulder he gave her while he stared out that window, which was all he did, except for when he was on top of her. He was weird. A real Count Screwloose, even if he was good-looking in a Robert Taylor kind of way.

She paused at the door, before going out, telling him she'd be at the Tap again tonight.

He turned his head toward her, his blue eyes cold and unblinking; he said nothing—didn't even shrug. Creepy.

"See ya," she said, and went out, his gaze still on her.

And that was why Harlen Maguire, standing watch, did not see Michael Sullivan, Sr., cross the street and go into the hotel.

For a town this size, the lobby of the Hotel Geneva was spacious and opulent, in a vaguely decadent, late-nineteenth-century way, potted ferns and plush furnishings and an elaborate mahogany check-in desk, behind which a harried fellow in pince-nez eyeglasses was talking on the phone. In a dark suit and tie, with a gold breast badge giving his name in small letters and MANAGER in bigger ones, the poor guy was dealing with a difficult guest.

"The chef isn't available, sir. . . . Can I help you?"

Sullivan paused just long enough to eye the key rack, where most of the keys were back on their hooks, their businessmen guests up and out of here. One hook, however—labeled 311 BRIDAL SUITE—was empty.

"Mr. Rance, I'm writing it down," the manager said.

Sullivan paused.

The manager was continuing. "Runny eggs, yes, sir. . . . You do not want your bacon to break off, I understand. . . . Right away, sir."

The hotel was old enough not to have elevators,

and Sullivan trotted up the central stairway to the mezzanine, where he found more stairs, which he climbed to the top floor, the third.

At room 311, the bridal suite, Sullivan glanced around at the otherwise empty corridor, withdrew his .45 from his right-hand coat pocket, and knocked with his left.

"It's *open!*" an irritated voice called from within.

Gun poised, Sullivan went in. The living room of the suite was expansive and expensive—chintz and crystal, overstuffed sofas and chairs, woodwork, washed ivory. At a room service table—its silver tray arrayed with a plate of a largely uneaten breakfast of boiled eggs in twin silver cups and crisscrossing crisp bacon—a man in a silk dressing robe stood pouring himself a cup of coffee, his back to Sullivan.

"Top marks for speed," the man said, his manner fussy and patronizing. "No marks for cookery."

Dripping with indignation, Alexander Rance turned and held up an egg in its silver cup. "*What* may I ask do you call . . . *this?*"

Rance's eyes were on the egg in the silver cup as he spoke, but his peripheral vision caught something that drew his attention to the man standing before him . . .

. . . pointing a .45 automatic at his head.

Sullivan said, "Put the egg down, Mr. Rance."

Rance's eyes showed white all around.

Sullivan said nothing, but his .45 spoke volumes.

Rance did as he'd been told, muttering apologetically.

But at least the accountant made no pretension of not recognizing his unexpected guest, settling down finally, acknowledging him with "Mr. Sullivan."

"Mr. Rance."

A plush pinkish-red brocade sofa was between them. The accountant held his hands high; his eyebrows were almost as high as he asked, "How did you find me?"

Sullivan said, "This is the best hotel in the area, and you're so very particular. Anyway, my colleagues in the banking business told me where to find you."

Not taking his eyes off the accountant for longer than a second, Sullivan went to the door, which had the key in it; he then locked the room, and crossed to the bedroom door, opening it, leaning in, gun ready. He quickly scanned the room—large double bed and floral brocade wallpaper; though no maid had been here yet, Rance had made his bed, at the foot of which was a large metal steamer-type trunk that was clearly not part of the bridal suite's florid furnishings.

Looking down his nose, Rance asked, "May I ask you to lower the weapon?"

Sullivan did.

"Thank you," Rance said with exaggerated distress. "Now what do you want?"

"Information."

The accountant would have had to bring along ledgers and record books, if they were going to close out all those accounts. Sullivan wanted them.

At first Rance seemed amused by the request. What good would such files do Sullivan?

And Sullivan admitted they wouldn't do *him* much good—but the feds who were readying indictments against Al Capone would really be able to use them.

Rance was shaking his head. Sullivan was completely out of his arena—Rance was strictly a man of books and numbers. . . .

That was fine with Sullivan, because that was what he wanted: the books with the numbers.

"I can't give you the files!"

Sullivan raised the .45 and cocked it—the click made its small, deadly point.

"All right! All right . . . they're in the next room."

The accountant stepped inside the adjacent bedroom. Sullivan remained in the living room, watching the man carefully through the open doorway. Rance pointed down at the large metal trunk, saying, "They're in here," meaning the files.

Sullivan, still in the outer room, gestured with the gun. "Bring it in."

Rance, understandably nervous, glanced past Sullivan toward a window onto the street. Sullivan noted this, and as Rance began dragging the trunk into the living room, leaving the bedroom door open, Sullivan went to that window and closed the curtains.

In the boardinghouse across the way, Maguire had already perked up, several minutes before, real-

izing Rance was talking to someone. Half the time
the accountant would deal with room service and
other hotel staff by telephone, making their lives
miserable; so seeing Rance through the window
speaking to someone right there in his suite set off an
alarm bell.

And then Mike Sullivan was in the window, closing the curtains—perfectly framed there, if only for
a moment.

That Ford he'd spied earlier . . . maroon, but the
same make as the other one. Had they painted it?
Had he been asleep at the wheel?

These and other thoughts rocketed through
Maguire's mind as he dressed quickly but with his
typical methodical precision, omitting his tie. Under
the bed he had stowed a canvas bag, and from this
he withdrew a long-barreled pump-action rifle.
Bowler atop his head, the rifle concealed under his
topcoat, he flew down the stairs and strode across
the street, paying little heed to the downtown traffic,
which was light anyway in this hick burg.

As he headed toward the entrance of the hotel, he
didn't even look up when a car screeched its brakes,
swerving to avoid him.

Someone else looked up though: Michael—who
had gotten bored on his watch and started reading
his Lone Ranger book, missing the sight of Maguire
passing right by on the driver's side of the Ford—
was now startled back into vigilance by the sound of
squealing brakes. In the driver's-side-door mirror,

he could see the man in the bowler hat jogging across the street.

The boy hadn't seen the gunman at that diner very well, but his father had described the man in detail and, besides, the snout of a rifle was sticking down like a skinny third leg that didn't quite reach the ground.

The man in the bowler was approaching the hotel, now, and Michael slammed his hand into the horn—twice.

The sounds made the man glance back, but he didn't make eye contact with Michael; and then the man was inside the hotel.

Heart racing, Michael hit the horn again, and again. He paused and repeated the action, and kept it up, getting scared, holding the horn down for a long time, so long that people on the street were stopping and staring.

But where was his father? Why hadn't the sounds sent him running out of the hotel?

About the time Maguire was reaching under the bed for the bag with his pump-action rifle in it, Sullivan was in the bridal suite, keeping his .45 trained on Alexander Rance, who was huffing and puffing as he pushed the large metal trunk out of the bedroom.

Rance glanced at the window, where Sullivan had shut the curtains, asked him to open them back up, complaining, "I won't be able to see!"

There was no overhead light, but several of the

crystal lamps were on. Sunlight filtering in through the closed curtains cast an eerie glow.

Sullivan ignored the request, saying, "Move."

Rance continued to push the apparently heavy trunk into the room. "What do you think you're going to accomplish by interfering with our business, Mr. Sullivan?"

"This has nothing to do with your business."

Breathing hard, still pushing the trunk, nearer the light of the lamps by the couch, Rance said, "It's all business—that's what you fail to grasp—and in business you must have something valuable to trade."

Those files would be a start, Sullivan thought.

"Especially"—the accountant grunted as he pushed the trunk—"for anyone as valuable as Connor Rooney."

Sullivan frowned. "I don't understand," he said. What made Connor Rooney valuable?

Rance's expression clouded, as if he'd said too much, bantering with this intruder.

A mechanical chatter—loud as hell!—drew Sullivan's attention away from Rance, who was rising from his crouch, the trunk pushed to the center of the room, now.

"Opening bell on Wall Street," Rance explained, nodding across the room.

In the shadow of an alcove, a ticker-tape machine stood, spewing tape, making a racket like a miniature machine gun. Under the glass jar covering the machine, a pile of yesterday's tape was strewn.

The machine's chatter was loud enough to blot away the outside world—including the sound of Sullivan's son, desperately honking the horn.

"Come on," Sullivan said. "Open it."

Rance withdrew a big ring of keys from his dressing-gown pocket, sorting through them, muttering, "Now which one is it?"

Sullivan gestured impatiently with the gun.

The accountant knelt at the trunk, tried the key. "No . . . it's not that one. . . ."

Sullivan threatened, and Rance insisted he was doing his best. Here was the key! "No, I tried that one. . . ."

Fumbling, the accountant dropped the keys to the carpet.

"Mr. Rance . . . do I look like a patient man?"

Rance threw a glare at Sullivan; that tone wasn't helping. "Oh, dear . . . better start again."

"Come on," Sullivan said, "come on. . . ."

"No . . . not that one. . . ."

Sullivan went over and jammed the gun into the accountant's left temple and said, "You've got one more try."

Rance selected another key and said, "Ah, here it is," inserted it into the keyhole and, with a click, unlocked the trunk. Sullivan took a step around, to get a look inside, as Rance opened the lid . . .

. . . on emptiness.

At that moment the ticker tape ran out, its chattering ceased, and the blurt of the car horn—the signal repeated over and over—finally made itself known to Sullivan.

Rance took that opportunity to scramble into the bedroom, slamming the door and locking it behind him.

And Mike Sullivan—with a second futile glance at the bare inside of the "heavy" trunk the accountant had struggled with so—knew he'd been set up. Rance had been the bait, and he knew he was the mouse . . . so where was the fucking cat?

A gunshot trumped the car horn, punching a hole through the bridal suite door—a rifle blast at close range!—splintering the wood. The honeymoon was over.

Sullivan took cover behind the trunk, its metal lid up, as somebody kicked in the door with a forceful boot heel, wood crunching, metal snapping, and the man in the bowler filled the doorway and—not seeing Sullivan—fired off five loud sharp shots in quick succession all around the room, including the bedroom door and wall.

Two shots slammed into the open metal lid, which was providing a shield of sorts for Sullivan, who stayed down as low as possible, the body of the trunk serving as better cover.

As the man with the rifle paused to reload, stepping inside what appeared to be an empty room, Sullivan popped up from behind the trunk and blasted away with the .45. But he'd been shooting somewhat blindly, and the slugs thudded into the sofa near the door as the guy with the rifle, losing his bowler, scrambled behind an end table that supported a crystal-shaded lamp, crouching there to finish reloading.

Sullivan, huddled low behind the trunk, could see where the two slugs had dimpled the lid; breathing hard, he mentally counted how many rounds he had left as time itself seemed to pause, and the room took on a ghostly silence broken only by the sound of his opponent reloading the rifle. In the wall and the door to the bedroom into which Rance had fled, daylight was slanting through bullet holes like swords in a magician's box. Dust motes floated. Crystal lamps stood mute and the elegant surroundings seemed at odds with the conflict at hand.

Sullivan didn't see his adversary pop up from behind the end table, but the punch of the bullets from the rifle—two more rounds—pounded into the trunk, which slammed into Sullivan, knocking him backward and to one side, robbing him of cover. The second he realized he was exposed, Sullivan squeezed off three fast rounds, and one of them shattered the crystal lamp on the end table, showering his opponent with flying shards of glass, hitting him right in the face, like a dozen terrible bee stings.

The gunman screamed in pain and surprise, and dropped to his knees. Sullivan, still on his side on the floor, out in the open, kept firing with the .45, though his bullets only served to send his bleeding moaning adversary seeking refuge behind the overstuffed sofa.

And then Sullivan was clicking on empty chambers, and he got a glimpse of the man with the rifle cowering behind the sofa, his bloody face in one hand, the rifle impotent—at least for the moment—in the other.

Sullivan took the opportunity to get to his feet and run over to the bedroom door, and—in a panel that had bullet holes punched through it already—kicked, then kicked again, letting daylight flood in. Then he reached in and around and turned the key in the lock.

Pushing into the room, Sullivan quickly turned, staying in a crouch, in case the man with the rifle advanced on him; he slammed a fresh clip in his .45, and as he backed in, he finally saw Rance—flung on the bed, on his back, his eyes and mouth open, and a pool of red on the silk robe, a spray of scarlet on the headboard and wall. One of the rifle slugs had caught the accountant, and taught Rance a final lesson about the business of crime.

Sullivan almost stumbled over something, and he looked down and saw a small black strongbox amid a scattering of file folders and accordion envelopes next to the bed. Too much stuff to grab up and carry . . . but the strongbox had a tiny label that said something big: CHIEF ACCOUNTS.

With his left hand, Sullivan grabbed the strongbox by its little handle, his right hand still ready to send death flying at that bleeding bastard in the next room.

The bedroom had a separate exit, and Sullivan took it, running down the corridor. On the second floor he found a window out onto a fire escape that brought him to the alley; and within seconds he was sprinting across the main street, toward where Michael was parked.

He didn't realize that Harlen Maguire had managed to stagger to the window and draw back the curtains and, pulling a revolver from his topcoat pocket, blinking away blood—no shards in his eyes, one small miracle—took aim.

Michael had spotted Papa, exiting that alley, and threw the Ford into reverse, backing the car toward his advancing father, neither of them wasting any time. But two gunshots discouraged them—holes punched in the roof of the car, sunlight streaming in!—and the boy heard his father yell, "Go! Go!"

And Michael knew not to disobey his father. He changed gears, as professional as any outlaw wheelman, and began to pull away, his father running alongside the car. The boy's reach wasn't long enough to open the door for his father, but Papa managed to get the door open himself, and was almost inside when another gunshot rang out, and Papa's shoulder flinched, even as he winced from the impact and pain.

Still, Papa somehow flung himself in the car, and he shut the door, yelling again, "Go! Go!"

Frightened as he was, knowing his father had been shot, Michael did his job, hitting the accelerator, speeding and winding and weaving in and around and through the morning traffic as sirens wailed behind him.

On the outskirts of town, he allowed himself to look at his father, who was holding on to his left shoulder with fingers that had blood seeping through them, making red trails down his hand.

Sullivan could see the panic on his boy's face, and he snapped, "I'm okay! I'm okay. . . . Watch the road."

The boy drove.

And in the bridal suite, Harlen Maguire dropped to his knees, as if about to pray, only he didn't clasp his hands; he held them before him, palms up. In the other room, through the open door, the corpse of Alexander Rance beckoned.

But Maguire didn't have his camera. And he was busy looking at his hands, anyway—the hands that had been holding his poor glass-ravaged face, hands covered in blood, dripping with red, and he was startled. It was as if all the blood he had on his hands was finally showing.

15

The only time we made the papers was the shooting at the Grand Hotel in Stillwater, when witnesses indeed saw me fleeing the scene at the wheel of the Ford, my father slumped over on the rider's side.

At the time, my father was painted as a homicidal thief who murdered a respectable accountant—one Alexander Rance—robbing him of hundreds of thousands of dollars from his rooms at Stillwater's Grand Hotel. In truth, my father took no money at all, merely records—ledger books and files.

At the time, of course, my father and I had other, more pressing concerns than our image in the newspapers— chiefly, survival. Fortunately for us, other families—perhaps most families—in those hard times were scratching out a modest living and knew what it was to struggle just to exist.

They are gone now, and their deeds—whether interpreted negatively or positively—cannot harm these good Samaritans. I would ask that you think of them as representative of a breed of American who lives no longer—

hearty pioneers who managed to wrest a livelihood of sorts out of hardscrabble land.

Farming in the Great Plains never really made a recovery after the collapse of farm prices in 1920 and '21. Though even worse adversity lay ahead—droughts and dust storms would soon place Kansas, Nebraska, and Oklahoma in the middle of the so-called Dust Bowl—farmer families were already barely scratching out a living after the Depression drove prices into the cellar.

Thus the landscape into which I drove my wounded father was topsoil rich and money poor, a desolate paradise that promised us, if not salvation, respite from the road.

Frightened though he was, Michael could handle the situation as long as his father was conscious, giving him directions—*turn here, stay at the speed limit, take a left.* Papa had managed to get the bleeding stopped with a piece of cloth torn from his own shirt, and wouldn't even let the boy stop to help wrap the makeshift bandage around himself.

That may have been what finally taxed his father's considerable stamina and willpower, sending this weakened strong man into unconsciousness.

And then panic rose in the boy like water overtaking a sinking ship. Instinctively, he pulled off the main road, knowing he had to find a residence, a farm maybe, to seek help for his father. The Ford did well on the rutted dirt road, but Michael had to slow, not wanting the jolts to cause his father pain, even in his unconscious state.

Up ahead were some rickety buildings—a farmhouse, a barn, shacklike structures constructed of paint-peeling planks—that might normally have put the boy off. Right now, he was happy to see any sign of civilization, even if this spread was more like the hillbilly houses he'd seen in the moving pictures and funny papers than the nice farms around Rock Island.

A pair of old people—in their fifties, maybe—were working in a field that looked pretty rough. It was warmer here, spring easing out winter, already. The couple was moving along slowly, kneeling at tilled soil, the man digging, the woman planting; their clothes were old and worn: the man in overalls and a ragged shirt and raggedy hat, the woman in a faded calico dress—both she and the dress had probably been pretty once, before the boy was born.

Michael pulled up at the edge of the field, where the couple worked, the boy thrilled to see any human being, particularly any who wasn't shooting at him and his father. He ran between tilled rows, desperately waving his arms, and the couple glanced at each other, knowing help was needed, ready to give it.

What followed was a frenzied blur to the boy—a heated knife digging at his delirious father's shoulder, a bloody bullet dropping into a tin cup like a coin in the offering plate at church, his father shivering with fever on a makeshift cot in the front room of the shacklike house.

Night sweats, according to the farmer. His name was Bill; he had kind blue eyes, a grooved face, and mostly white hair. It was a good thing, his father sweating the poison out, the farmer told Michael; stay with your pa, son. . . .

Michael didn't have to be told that. His father had tended to him over these long weeks, and now he removed his father's shirt, unbuttoning cuffs that were frayed and stained from their travels. He folded his father's tie, placing it over the end of the cot, ritualistically, in the way he'd seen his papa do so many times.

The farmer and his wife—her name was Virginia, and she had blue eyes, too, in a face as pleasant as it was weathered, and dark blonde graying hair—stayed in the room, but out of the way, mostly over by the kitchen part. They wore concern in their features that seemed unusual to Michael, considering he and his father were strangers. They didn't have Catholic icons in their house, so they weren't of the faith of his family; but Michael knew these were Christians, because they did Christian things . . . unlike some people who said they believed in Jesus.

By the next night, his father was awake, but groggy, still not really communicating very well. Michael sat beside him and fed him soup with a spoon that was a little too small for the job; he would have to wipe Papa's mouth with a frayed napkin Mrs. Baum had provided. It was as if Papa were the child, and Michael the father, and the change felt good, made the boy feel older, that he was somehow paying his papa back for all the wonderful things his father had done for him.

When the Baums had gone off to their own bedroom, Michael settled on the threadbare sofa opposite his father's cot—Papa was still feverish, but not as bad, not nearly as bad—and the boy was settling his head on a pillow Mrs. Baum had given him, when he noticed the gun in the holster under his father's jacket, on a chair where Mr. Baum had draped it.

Papa was asleep, and so was the farm couple. The boy crept off the sofa, carefully removed the gun from the holster, and he stood and looked down at the weapon, huge in his small hand—rough and cold, not smooth and warm, like you'd imagine, from Tom Mix and the Lone Ranger.

Sullivan was not exactly sure how many days had passed. Three at least, probably no more than five. Unshaven, topcoat over his tieless white shirt, he sat in an old wicker chair on the porch of the timeworn farmhouse, feeling better, a tin cup of steaming coffee cradled nicely in his hands. In the world around him, green was overtaking brown, and the snow was gone. When had spring crept up on them? It had been winter just an eye blink ago.

Yet somehow it was not a surprise. They had been on the road together, he and Michael, forever—and yet there was no way to put enough time and space between them and the taking of Annie and Peter, to give any solace, to make it seem anything but terrible and fresh in his memory.

Out in the field—what a hard life these people had, but it was a life better than their own at present—Bill was allowing Michael to help in the planting, the boy doing the digging with energy and enthusiasm, while the warmly amused farmer followed along, dropping seeds.

Mrs. Baum, a grizzled goddess in a frayed checkered dress, was watching the boy, too, as she peeled potatoes. Then she glanced toward the ramshackle barn, where the maroon Ford could be glimpsed, the door half off its hinges.

"When are you headin' out?" she asked.

Sullivan knew what she meant.

"We've stayed long enough," he said. "Don't want to cause you any trouble."

"No trouble so far."

Sullivan thanked the woman for not asking questions; she and her husband had taken them in, strangers—bullet holes in their car, a bullet in him.

A smile grooved her face, a thousand smile lines joining it. Mrs. Baum, her smile almost glowing, nodding toward Michael, said, "He's a good worker."

Nodding, Sullivan felt a smile of his own blossom—he was enjoying his son's antics out in the field. He asked the woman, "You have any kids?"

"Nah, we met too late." This *was* a family farm, though; it had belonged to her husband's people, and had once been "right somethin' to see." No, no children, she shrugged. "Can't have it all."

These people had next to nothing, Sullivan thought; and yet they were grateful for their lot in life.

Almost too casually, the woman said, "He dotes on you."

Sullivan looked at her, surprised by the remark.

She turned her smile on the confused father. "You don't see it?"

Frankly, he didn't, and just shrugged by way of response; but the next moment, his eyes caught Michael's, the boy looking up from his work, joy in his face, and he threw a casual wave at his father, before returning to his digging.

Sullivan did not understand the wave of emotion. It came up somewhere deep inside of him, rolling with an awful warmth up his chest into his face and moisture welled behind his eyes, overtaking him. He excused himself and went back into the house.

He did not want these kind people to see him weep, nor did he want his son to witness that shameful action.

Michael awoke on the sofa, startled out of sleep by a dreadful dream.

In the dream—the nightmare—he'd been in the Rooney mansion, and he and his father were kneeling at the coffin again, like at the wake. But when Michael peeked inside the box, his father was inside—with pennies on his eyes! And when Michael looked to his side, where a moment before Papa had been kneeling, too—it was Mr. Rooney now, smiling in that grandfatherly way, his arm around him. Then the boy ran away and Mr. Rooney started to chase him; at some point Mr. Rooney turned into Connor Rooney and then Michael ran into a room and it was the bathroom of their own house, white tile and red blood and dead Peter and dead Mama and he made himself wake up.

He stumbled over in his pajamas to where his father sat at a table, going over books and records in the light of a kerosene lamp. Papa was in his T-shirt and suspenders and trousers, his bandaged arm showing, blood dried there, a reddish brown.

Papa looked like he was having trouble—it reminded the boy of himself, trying to do his schoolwork, really struggling.

When Michael approached, Papa looked up—the boy had been expecting reproval for not being asleep, but instead his father's expression was warm, the man obviously pleased to see him.

That really helped, after the nightmare.

"Hello," Papa said.

"I had a bad dream."

"Wanna talk about it?"

The boy shook his head.

His father pulled out the chair next to him at the table. "Come and sit down . . . if you want."

Michael sat. The papers his father was going over were figures, numbers in columns and rows.

"Math, huh?" the boy said, making a face.

Papa smiled at him. "Yeah—I always hated it."

"Me, too," Michael said, and grinned.

Then his father stopped and he had a funny look—almost like he felt guilty about something. "What subjects do you like . . . did you like . . . at school?"

That came out of left field! The boy thought for a few moments, then said, "Bible history, maybe."

This seemed to really surprise Papa. "Why?"

He shrugged. "I like the stories."

His father thought about that; then he nodded.

"Peter was good at math," Michael said.

This also seemed to be news to Papa. "Was he?"

Michael nodded. "Did you like Peter more than me?"

His father's expression was blank; but something in the man's eyes made Michael wish he hadn't asked the question.

"No, Michael," he said, smiling, and he touched the boy's arm. "I loved you both the same."

"But you were different with me."

"Was I?"

The boy nodded.

His father sighed, looking puzzled and trying to find the words. Finally he said, "Well, maybe that's because Peter . . . well, he was just a sweet boy. You know? Just sweet.

"And you . . ."

Michael watched his father's face as the man searched for the words.

Then Papa said, "You were more like me. And I didn't want you to be."

The boy thought about that.

Then his father said, "I didn't mean to be different."

This was getting hard on both of them, so Michael

just shrugged and said, "Okay. It's okay. . . . 'Night, Pa."

And on impulse, he hugged his father around the neck, being careful not to hurt the man's sore arm. Papa hugged back, not being so careful.

After his son began softly snoring on the couch, Sullivan was able to get his mind back on the task before him. Something Rance had said—or maybe it was something about the accountant's attitude—made Sullivan think an answer of sorts might be waiting to be found in these figures.

So he sorted through the documents, setting some aside, looking at others, overwhelmed, out of his element. Finally a buff-colored file almost seemed to appear in his hands.

CONNOR ROONEY, it was boldly marked.

Surprised, interested, he began to look carefully through it—at letters, accounts, bills of lading, receipts, dockets, and more. He pushed the other books and ledgers and files aside and concentrated on this one.

And when the sun came up, Sullivan—fully dressed, ready to ride, .45 under his arm, new information in his brain—gently shook Michael awake, saying, "Get up. Get your things."

The bleary-eyed boy leaned on an elbow and asked, "What's the rush?"

"We're leaving." They didn't want to wear out their welcome, did they?

Michael gave him no argument, though the boy was clearly conflicted about leaving behind his new "family," and yet obviously anxious to get back out on the road with his father.

As they rolled out of the barn in the Ford, Sullivan waved at the farm couple, who waved back. He leaned out the window and said, "We left a little thank-you," and pointed to the barn. Then the car rolled out onto, and down, the dirt road.

The Baums were already heading into the barn, and Sullivan smiled at his son, who smiled back. The couple would soon find out it sometimes paid to be hospitable: the Sullivan "gang" had left them a satchel full of money and a note that simply read, "Thank you."

They were on a paved highway when he told the boy they were heading back to the Tri-Cities.

Something didn't add up, he told his son, nodding toward the back, where the ledger books and files were now stowed in the compartment under the seat. Men lied, but numbers didn't.

The boy still didn't understand.

"It's all in the math," his father said.

16

Though I have no direct proof other than my recollection, I believe my father had heard from a friend on Rooney's payroll that the old man was packing up for a New Mexico "vacation." This was in part why we rushed from Oklahoma back to Illinois, while Papa was still weak from his injury.

That, and the discovery he had made in that strongbox he'd taken from the suite of Alexander Rance.

A sunny Sunday morning, crisp but not quite cold, found the bells ringing and the Irish Catholics of the Illinois side of the Tri-Cities converging on St. Peter's. The parking lot was full outside, the pews full within. God was doing a hell of a business today, John Rooney thought, eyeing the throng—better business than he had, of late, his mind on this goddamned Sullivan matter.

Rooney—along with his trusted bodyguards, Jimmy and Sean (on his right and left hand respectively), as well as other more respectable members of the parish—knelt at the altar rail, to receive communion. Among the morning's last group to receive the Eucharist, Rooney rose and returned down the aisle, the congregation all around kneeling in their pews in meditation. The choir sang in the Latin gibberish that the old man found so soothing—all this ritual was reassuring, the pomp and circumstance of it such wonderful theater, the trappings a delightful blend of fear and forgiveness, mass itself a droning reiteration of tradition and order in a cruel, chaotic world.

John Rooney had no use for the empty cross of the Protestants, who insisted their Christ had risen, and that the cross should be a symbol of redemption. He embraced instead the cross of the Catholics, with Jesus in plain view, suffering, bleeding, living the life of hell-on-earth His Father had willed to man.

Rooney sidled into his pew, and with Jimmy and Sean's help lowered himself to the padded kneeling bench; moments later—in the row behind him—a man spoke, not in a whisper, but softly enough that only Rooney (and perhaps his boys) would hear.

"Hello, John."

Rooney did not need to turn to know Mike Sullivan knelt at the bench in the pew directly in back of him.

Sullivan nodded to Rooney's bodyguards. "Sean, Jimmy. Morning."

Rooney, almost smiling, said, "You're a smart man, Michael."

Neutral ground—sanctuary.

Rooney asked, "What do you want?"

"I want to talk. . . . Downstairs."

Rooney sensed the man behind him standing, and he got to his feet—batting off the help of his chow-derheaded bodyguards—and, with a nod to Sean to let him pass, moved out of the pew. In a brown suit that looked somewhat the worse for wear, Sullivan stood waiting for Rooney to fall in alongside him, and the two bodyguards followed as the two men moved together up the aisle toward the church entrance. Around them heads were bowed, as Latin call and response echoed throughout the cavernous church and sunlight filtered in colorfully through stained glass.

Near the front doors, to the left, were stairs that went down into the basement. Then the little group, footsteps ringing off cement, was in a corridor, off of which a large room could be used for various meetings and even banquets; Michael Sullivan, Jr., had attended a birthday party in that very room, the night the boy's brother was killed in his stead.

Rooney nodded to Sean and Jimmy to wait outside, and he and his former chief enforcer went through a small door into another room. Sullivan snapped on the lights, a few bare hanging bulbs exposing in their yellowish glow an unfinished windowless concrete area that had a cryptlike atmosphere, littered with religious artifacts, some of them stored, others just abandoned.

The old man and his younger ex-associate stood facing each other—no chairs were available, though they might have used one of the pews stacked around, amid kneeling benches, various plaster saints, and a bloody Jesus on the cross leaning against the wall, a bystander with more on His mind than the two of them.

Rooney had a flash of the basement of his home, and the last good time he'd had with his two god-sons, playing dice, rolling the "bones" against the concrete wall, losing to Peter. He was still losing to Peter, after all these weeks.

Above them the muffled sound of mass made the Latin even more indecipherable, providing a strange, otherworldly accompaniment to their conversation.

Rooney's chest swelled; seeing Mike Sullivan—his other son, the better son—filled him with emotion, much of it contradictory: love, hate, pride, shame.

"I didn't think I'd see you again." Rooney said, let-ting the brogue roll. He flinched as Sullivan thrust something toward him: a file, a manila folder, stuffed with papers and such.

"Read this," Sullivan said.

Rooney did not reach for the file his former soldier offered him. Sullivan tossed the file to the floor in front of Rooney's feet. "It's all in here—Connor's been working for Chicago."

Seemed whenever Rooney had turned down something as beneath his dignity—narcotics, forcible white slaving, union racketeering—Connor had gone right ahead with it, with Capone's blessing.

Above them, Latin droned.

"Connor's been stealing from you for years," Sullivan said. "He's kept accounts open under the names of dead men—men like the McGoverns."

Rooney shook his head—he wasn't hearing this.

"I stood there," Sullivan said through his teeth, "and helped him kill Fin . . . to line his own pockets. I thought I was working for you, John . . . but I wasn't."

Finally the old man said, "So you think I'd give up my son?"

"He was betraying you."

Rooney locked eyes with him—the old man's gaze was blue ice. "I . . . *know*."

The simple statement almost knocked Sullivan back.

The old man was smiling bitterly, shaking his head again, as if disagreeing with himself. *Of course* Rooney knew—he knew what Connor had done, and what Connor was.

Michael Sullivan had not expected this response from the old man. Right now he felt as if he'd been struck a blow to the belly. This had been his last effort, one final chance to get through to the one man who could end the nightmare.

The old man's face was a wrinkled mask of intensity, his blue eyes cold and yet blazing. "Now listen to me! I tried to avoid more bloodshed—you wouldn't accept it, so I did what was necessary. . . ."

Sullivan had loved this old man like a father.

And as if reading Sullivan's mind, Rooney said, "I've always loved you like a son. . . . I'm telling you to leave! Before it's too late."

Above them, the congregation said, "*Ah-men!*"

Hadn't the old man made it clear? Sullivan could leave this town, this country, with his remaining son, to live long happy lives. Open a shop, buy a farm, or sit back and spend Capone's money till Gabriel calls.

Or?

"If you stay here," the old man said, looking at him gravely, "you know how it ends."

Sullivan felt he was talking to a brick wall, whose response to whatever he said was to fall on him; but he had to try again—he and this man had been close, so very close, and their heart-to-heart talks had gone long into many nights.

"*Think*, John—they're protecting him now . . . but when you're gone, they're not going to need him."

Sullivan pointed at Rooney. "It ends the same way no matter what—with Connor dead!"

Rooney's smile was like a skeleton's. "That may be. But you're asking me to give you the keys to his room so you can walk in, put a gun to his head, and pull the trigger. I can't do that."

Quietly, as if praying, Sullivan said, "He murdered Annie . . . and Peter."

The reminder of his dead godson and his dead godson's mother seemed to give Rooney pause.

But Rooney wouldn't let him get away with that. How many men had Sullivan killed? Did he imagine they didn't each have a wife? Children? A mother, a father? Didn't Danny McGovern have a brother? Who were these men they had killed, Sullivan and Rooney—clay figures? Phantoms? Or men who lived and breathed, until they took that away from them, forever?

Rooney's eyes and nostrils flared; his false teeth flashed. "There are *only* murderers in this room. . . . Open your eyes, Mike! This is the life we lead . . . the life we chose. . . . There's only one guarantee. None of us will see heaven."

Muffled Latin filled the silence.

Then Sullivan said, "Michael could." Someday, many years from now, Michael might join his boy Peter in heaven, with his mother.

Rooney winked at him. "Then do everything you can to make sure that happens. Take it, Mike. Leave . . . I'm begging you. It's the only way out."

For the first time Sullivan considered the possibility of taking Rooney at his word.

Rooney sensed this, and took the opening: Mike would go with his blessing, and take the money he'd stolen with him. Yes, Rooney knew Sullivan had stolen a lot; but Rooney had a lot—he would replace it.

"And *if* I don't?"

Sullivan stared at the old man; the old man stared back.

"Then I'll mourn the son *I* lost," Rooney said and turned to leave.

Sullivan wondered if this was more self-serving blarney, or if it came from Rooney's heart; then he had a sudden revelation: *the answer to that question didn't matter!* When the time had come to choose between loyalty and blood, between sentiment and

blood, even money and blood, Rooney had chosen
blood.

As he stepped from the room, backing out into the
corridor with his .45 drawn, keeping a close eye on
Sean and Jimmy, Sullivan could not shake that
thought: *Rooney had chosen blood.*

And by the time he slipped away from the sanctuary of the church—the mass loud now, muffled no
more, though still its arcane Latin self—Sullivan
knew what had to be done.

17

My father is buried next to my mother and brother now; and one day I will join them there in the same cemetery. Connor Rooney is buried there, too. When I first heard, I thought that was a terrible thing—even the ground should be more discriminating.

I've come to see the rightness of it. We were bound together in life and death, all of us, and my father, mother, and brother will be forever linked to the Rooneys, as will I.

The Paradise Hotel was in downtown Prophetstown, near the Tri-Cities, on the way to Chicago. Nondescript, almost run-down, the three-story frame building was anything but paradise, the kind of lodgings the less successful traveling salesmen resorted to in these hard times.

The boy was pretending to sleep in his clothes on top of one of the twin beds in a room whose yellowish wainscoted walls had grime and stains from the decades that had passed since the hotel's heyday. A naked bulb screwed in the wall provided the only illumination; Sullivan switched it off and sat on the bed next to the boy. Rain streaked the windows, and its reflected shimmer made patterns on the child. Thunder rumbled, sounding distant, but a threat nonetheless.

Sullivan was in the same suit he'd worn to the church today. He wore no tie. This was the end of the road and he knew it—and he knew what had to be done, knew now the only way that Capone and Nitti would give up Connor to him.

Because he had phone calls to make, and other preparations, Sullivan had taken the adjoining room, as well; and he'd made his arrangement with the desk clerk for the long-distance calls.

In that adjoining room, he sat at a table, a work area where salesmen and businessmen could go over their receipts and records, and used the phone. Shabby, sparsely furnished, these two rooms did not constitute a suite worthy of, say, Alexander Rance. But it suited Mike Sullivan's purposes just fine.

Glancing toward his father's room, the boy saw a strip of light along the doorway's edge. He rose and went to the door, nudging it open another crack, and peeked in.

His father sat at a table, the hard-shell black case before him, closed; like a master musician, he unsnapped the clasps, lifted the lid, and revealed the protectively nestled parts of his instrument—the tommy gun, which had been with them on their journey, but had gone as yet unused.

Michael was amazed by the speed, the precision of it: piece by piece, checking each one, his father assembled the gun quickly, efficiently, snapping the parts together, tiny loud mechanical clicks and clacks, each one making the boy flinch. Michael had seen his father like this many times on the road—intense, methodical, precise—but something seemed different tonight. Papa was preparing not just the gun, but himself—snapping his own parts together, somehow.

Steeling himself.

Finally, the drum of ammunition was clicked in place onto the assembled machine gun, and the boy went in.

Michael just stood there in his rumpled clothes and stared at his father with blank accusation. "What are you going to do?"

"Just one last thing," he said, surprised to see his son awake.

Then the boy asked him who he was going to kill.

Sullivan, not irritated, even gentle, said, "Go back to bed, Michael."

And nothing was left to say. The boy stumbled off to his bed, and the man took one last look at the machine gun before moving on to his Colt .45 automatic, which could use a cleaning.

Later, still seated at the table, he made out a list of banks and safe-deposit box numbers on a sheet of Paradise Hotel letterhead; he wrote "Michael" on an envelope and inserted a letter he had just written into that. Then he slipped in a fat wad of cash, enough to carry the boy for weeks, perhaps months, and licked the flap and sealed it shut.

Sullivan went back to where his son slept, and placed the envelope on the scarred nightstand, where a Lone Ranger book lay folded open next to the boy's small revolver. Again he stood beside Michael and looked at him for a long time—studying him, committing to memory every detail of the child, as if he hoped to recognize the boy in some other lifetime.

Then he stroked his son's hair, thinking how much he loved the child, hoping Michael knew, and got up and returned to the next room.

Alone in the room now, Michael eyed the letter on the nightstand suspiciously. The word "good-bye" seemed to rise off the envelope like steam.

For several hours that rainy evening, at the small restaurant in downtown Rock Island, not far from his newspaper office on Second Avenue, John Rooney met with certain key associates. Rooney was handling his own legal matters now, since the demise of Joe Kelly.

But even the boss got chased out at closing time, and as the restaurant staff piled chairs on tables, and lights winked off, the old man and his six young bodyguards (the seventh, Jimmy, had stayed with the Pierce-Arrow) shrugged into topcoats,

Sean plucking his umbrella from where it leaned against the wall, and prepared to head out into the storm. Outside the restaurant windows, the night was as dark as it was wet, raindrops streaming down in glimmering ribbons, the street black and shiny, as if freshly painted.

Thunder growled as Rooney stepped onto the sidewalk, rain pelting the umbrella Sean held for him. Sean and the other watchdogs had no umbrella of their own—the rain had at them, assailing them as they flanked their boss, their eyes searching the darkness, the downpour, for anything suspicious, any moving shape, any sign of life on streets where reasonable men had long since been driven indoors by the weather.

The two automobiles were parked down the street a bit—Rooney's Pierce-Arrow touring car, and the Velie sedan, for the bodyguard overflow— and the old man walked quickly, not anxious to get wet, his shoes and spats taking a shellacking as he strode through puddles. He paused at the car—did he hear something? Something other than the relentless raindrops?

He looked around, and so did Sean, and so did the others. Nothing. Just ovals of streetlamp light and pools of water making strange designs on the pavement as rain slanted down like a watery ambush.

Rooney waited for Jimmy to open the door; he could see his driver, behind the wheel, but not clearly, the rain-streaked window clouding the issue. Annoyed, Rooney tromped around to the driver's side, the bodyguards following, Sean keeping the old man covered with the umbrella—and shook the driver's door handle, saying, "Hey, Jimmy! Jimmy! Open the door, boy! Open the . . ."

His shaking of the locked door handle was just enough to prompt a reaction from Jimmy—who slumped forward onto the steering wheel, face tilted toward the side window. Even through the smear of rain, the dark red hole in Jimmy's forehead could be seen, as could the man's open, empty-staring eyes.

"Christ," Rooney said, stepping away from the grisly, ghostly sight.

And all around him his bodyguards drew their weapons, spreading out along the traffic-free street, eyes fanning the rain-swept darkness.

Rooney did not carry a gun—he left that to his men. And a small army of his soldiers were all around him. Sullivan would know what he'd be up against—so he'd killed Jimmy, as a warning, to spook Rooney, and fled into the night. The old man just about had himself convinced of that when thunder shook the night.

Not God's thunder: a Thompson submachine gun's.

All around Rooney, in rapid succession, his bodyguards—few of them even firing off shots of their own—were cut to pieces by a rain of lead, the chopper blazing orangely in the dark, sending his soldiers tumbling, stumbling, flopping, dancing, shaken like naughty children, blood mist puffing in the night. One by one these fierce men with guns splashed whimpering to the wet pavement, blood flowing into rain puddles, turning the street a glistening pink.

Rooney could not watch. Unarmed, he could not act. Trapped, he could not run. So he just stood there and stared at the pavement and listened to the ungodly roar of gunfire until it had stopped, only to echo through the empty streets of Rock Island.

And now, scattered all around him, his loyal boyos, this one on his belly, that one on his back, this man in the gutter, that man rolled into a ball, another with brains leaching out of his shattered skull like jelly . . . and Sean on his side, the umbrella just out of his grasp, as if he were reaching for it, the gun in his limp hand only half raised. Rain pounded the blood and the gore, diluting, then obliterating it; and lightning flashed and thunder clapped, and in a momentary flash of white, there stood Sullivan—down the street—with the Thompson in his hands.

Then, without moving, he disappeared into darkness.

Rooney waited. Why run? Mike had figured it, hadn't he? The only way to get Capone to give up Connor was if John Rooney were dead.

The old man could hear the footsteps on the wet pavement, growing closer, closer, and then Mike Sullivan—the machine gun in his right hand—was standing behind him, the two almost close enough to reach out to each other . . . but not quite.

Rooney turned, his chin jutted—trembled. Hadn't he been as much a father to Mike Sullivan as to his own boy?

But Sullivan knew the difference: *he wasn't blood.*

And now the old man realized, Sullivan needed Rooney's blood, to settle it. . . . Well, those who took this path always knew—didn't they? Someday, some night, they all might come to an end like this.

Sullivan raised the .45, his eyes brimming with tears.

But there was truth in his voice when Rooney said, "I'm glad it's you."

Sullivan shot him anyway, pumping bullet after bullet into Rooney's chest.

Rooney stumbled back into the Pierce-Arrow and slid down the side of the car, sat for a moment, then fell on his side. A stream of blood from his torso made its way toward the gutter.

Sullivan stood for several long moments, staring at the corpse of a man he had loved; he had wept over his dead wife and son, and for Michael, too, and he might have been weeping now, but the rain streaming down his face concealed it, even from himself.

Around him, in buildings on all sides, lights were going on in windows, yellow squares glowing in the dark wet night—then faces appeared in those squares, indistinct, smeary bystanders looking down on the carnage in silence from the warmth of their lodgings.

Only one man in the street was standing—the rest were scattered in various postures of violent death. He must have looked so small to them, Sullivan thought, viewed on from high, a man standing alone in the rainy street.

He looked up at them, his face moving from blurred face to blurred face, explaining himself . . . no, warning them of where life could take them.

And Mike Sullivan walked back into the rainy darkness, which swallowed him, leaving the empty street behind.

Though Frank Nitti's office was in the Lexington Hotel, he—unlike Capone—did not live on the premises; he'd come over from his home on the near West Side to be available when Sullivan called back.

With old man Rooney dead, Al wouldn't give a damn about Connor Rooney. . . . In fact, with both Rooneys gone, it opened the door wide in the Tri-Cities for the Capone Outfit. Too bad Sullivan was no longer interested in working for them—Sullivan was the best at his trade Nitti had ever encountered.

Right now, with most of the lights off, he sat at his desk, in his shirtsleeves and suspenders and no tie, taking his second call tonight from the remarkable Mr. Sullivan.

"John Rooney is dead," Sullivan's voice said

over the scratchy line, as cold and matter-of-fact as a nurse saying the doctor will see you now; the sound of clatter and chatter in the background indicated the man was calling from a restaurant or diner.

Sullivan did not expect any retaliation; he had taken down Rooney's seven best men, too—best after him, that is.

"What do you want?" Nitti said.

"Connor Rooney."

"I understand. But we want your assurance that after that . . . it's over."

"You both have that assurance. . . . My son and I will disappear."

"The Lexington Hotel. Room 1432."

And Nitti hung up.

Then the Chicago mob's top business executive— the real spider at the web's center—considered going home; it was, after all, late on a Sunday night, though his wife, Anna, would be asleep by now. Perhaps he should stay until Sullivan arrived at the hotel, and this nasty business was over. . . .

On reflection, this seemed to Nitti the prudent course of action, and he selected a file from a stack on the desk and, in a pool of yellow light from a desk lamp, went to work.

It had rained in Chicago, too, but on the drive from Rock Island, the downpour had faded to a drizzle and now it was a memory, the streets in the Loop taking on a slick, glisteny black sheen reflecting streetlamp glow and the neon of sleeping businesses, as if the pavement had caught occasional fire.

Sullivan parked down the block on Twenty-second, glad to be alone, pleased not to be making his boy part of this. The Thompson was in the car, in the backseat, still assembled; all he was carrying was a .45 in his shoulder holster and a .38 in his topcoat pocket. The wind picked up scraps of paper, which seemed to race across South Michigan Avenue, scrambling toward the Lexington Hotel. Sullivan took his time. He was in no hurry.

This endless night had been long coming.

No doorman was on duty, not in the wee hours of early Monday morning. And the lobby was nearly deserted—a hotel man at the front desk; and by the elevators, skinny, edgy, snappily dressed Marco, who'd been his armed elevator operator on Sullivan's last visit to the Lexington, seemed to be the only watchdog.

Sullivan nodded to Marco.

Marco nodded to Sullivan.

And the watchdog reached over and pressed the UP button for him; the grillwork doors opened, Marco stepped aside, and Sullivan stepped in. The doors closed, leaving an unconcerned Marco behind.

On the fourteenth floor, Sullivan exited the elevator, taking the corridor at left, following Nitti's instructions. His gloved hand was in his topcoat pocket clenching the .38 revolver. He moved down the empty corridor, glancing at doors, ready to react—trusting Nitti, but not trusting him.

At room 1432, the door stood ajar. The brawny watchdog from his previous visit—Harry—stood in the hall, waiting for Sullivan to arrive.

The two men nodded at each other, Harry standing aside as Sullivan entered the comfortably plush, well-appointed suite.

Sullivan gave Harry a look, and Harry nodded toward the bathroom door.

The Angel of Death made his way into the suite, approaching the door the watchdog had indicated.

He took a breath and pushed open the door, a bright white-tiled bathroom, larger than some whole apartments; the mirrors were fogged, the air thick with steam.

Sullivan was just standing looking down at the pale figure—a scrawny-looking naked man, such a pitiful creature to have caused such a fuss.

Then Connor sensed something and his eyes popped open and his sallow complexion paled even further, his mouth open as if frozen in midbreath.

Sullivan knew he should take his time killing the son of a bitch . . . but he just couldn't bear the man's company.

Connor's eyes narrowed when Sullivan shot him once in the chest, and again in the stomach.

Hell will be heaven, Sullivan thought, *if I can spend eternity making you pay for what you did to them.*

And Sullivan shot Connor in the head—just as he had the man's father.

The corpse dropped down into the soapy, blood-frothy water, the white tiles surrounding spattered and smeared with crimson.

Sullivan emerged. He walked down the corridor, staying alert, and put the gun back in his coat pocket.

Nitti was true to his word, and Sullivan's exit through the Lexington lobby was as uneventful as his arrival. Within minutes he was in the maroon Ford, heading back to his son.

Michael had slept very little. He never did put on his pajamas. He tried to read his Lone Ranger book, but the Lone Ranger just seemed . . . silly now. From time to time, he would kneel by his bed and pray for his father's welfare.

Michael had never sorted out his feelings about his godfather. The man had been like a grandpa to Peter and him, and in these long weeks, in the boy's mind, Mr. Rooney had become a sort of boogey-man . . . and yet the good images of his godfather remained in his memory.

When he heard the footsteps at the hall, he'd been sitting on the edge of the bed, eyes shut tight, praying for his father—at this point, just that his father would return. Never mind any of the rest of it.

And then he opened his eyes, the footsteps very near, surprised to see light coming in the window—dawn—and the key turned in the lock . . . and the door opened.

Papa.

Michael threw himself into his father's arms.

Had their embrace been any tighter, it would have hurt.

Michael closed his eyes, blinking away tears—and the brightness of the dawn. The way the sun was pouring in the window, you would never have known how hard it had rained last night.

18

My memories of the drive to Perdition may be less than trustworthy. Everything I remember prior to that day is a winter memory—largely in black and white, like old movie footage, or some people's dreams.

But the drive to Perdition, in my mind's eye, is in full color, dominated by the clear blue of the sky and the green of a world that had been bleak winter yesterday and was glorious spring today.

Surely these recollections are influenced by emotions and time—the last day of winter is not a dead thing, with the first day of spring an explosion of life.

Yet that is how I remember it.

I am, after all, the only one left. I'm in my winter now, recalling the spring day we drove to Perdition.

They had spoken little, on the first day of the trip to Perdition, but a new warmth seemed to bind them. Smiling like the child he still was, the boy was enjoying the spring day, drinking in the sun, hanging his head out the window, letting the wind skim over him and roar in his ears. That his son had retained a certain innocence after this ordeal was a small miracle—that the little revolver Sullivan had given Michael had never been used gave Sullivan strength, and hope.

They stayed at a motel in Missouri, knowing they would be at the lake by the next afternoon, evening at the latest. And now, gliding down paved roads—the sun was reflecting off the green leaves so brightly that the man had to stop and buy sunglasses—they began to talk. For the first time, the father and son seemed to share something beyond blood—they liked each other. They were comrades who had shared hardship and weathered adversity, who had helped each other through a difficult, even tragic time.

But there was nothing serious about their conversation, with only a few passing references to Annie or Peter. Michael asked him what it was like growing up as a boy in Ireland, for example; and Sullivan was only too glad to tell him. And somehow his son seemed instinctively to know not to ask about his combat experiences in the Great War. They both had had enough of their own war, in recent days.

Then Sullivan—feeling more than an occasional twinge of guilt over how little he really knew about the boy—would question his son about his likes and dislikes. He heard the entire story of how the Lone Ranger was the last of a band of Texas Rangers who had been "betrayed and bushwhacked by the Cavendish gang." He heard about Tom Mix, and Mickey Mouse, and Little Orphan Annie.

And he knew Michael had an interest in baseball, but had never seen him play—there'd been no organized games at the Villa—and it turned out, last summer, the boy had been playing shortstop with a bunch of guys informally. The diamond, Michael said, was over at Longview Park.

That cast a slight pall—Longview Park was on Twentieth Street, across from the Rooney mansion.

Later Michael asked his father about music. The boy approached this delicately, and finally Sullivan figured out why: Michael only knew his father could play the piano because of the duet Sullivan and Rooney had played at the McGovern wake.

Michael asked his father if he'd taken lessons, and Sullivan said no . . . he'd just picked it up. Playing by ear, it was called. You just sort of hit the keys and listened and remembered—his mother'd had a piano.

Michael's eyes were wide with interest. He had never met his grandmother. She had died on the other side of the ocean. The Atlantic.

Somehow it bound them further, this sudden realization that they both had lived lives filled with incident and interests; Sullivan looked forward to getting to know his son even better. And he could tell, from the boy's questions, that Michael felt the same.

By late afternoon of the second day they were on a rural gravel road, surrounded by startling foliage. Sullivan pulled up along the roadside, near a dirt trail through high grass leading to lush woods.

"We have to walk the rest of the way," Sullivan said, getting out.

Soon they were angling down a hillside—no top-coat for the father, no jacket for the son, in this invit-ing weather—emerging from the woods, where a beautiful if oddly desolate landscape awaited.

Dusk was dispensing shadows to soften the view, touching the stretch of beach along the lake with cool blue; a light breeze blew in off the lightly white-capped water. No sign of any car except a battered flivver that belonged to Aunt Sarah.

Looking toward the cabinlike house on the beach, Michael asked, "Is that it?"

"That's it," his father said.

"Hey . . ." Michael began, smiling. "I knew there was a dog."

From around the house a big golden retriever was loping, floppy ears and lolling tongue, a friendly conglomeration of breeds, whose tail was wagging at the sign of company. Michael ran to meet the dog, and immediately they began to play, running to-ward the beach.

Sullivan did not join them. He merely stood and watched his son behaving like the boy he was.

Forgive me, Annie, Sullivan thought prayerfully, *for the dangerous road I've taken him down.*

Then he headed on toward the house, allowing his son to caper on the beach with the hound. Up the porch and through the open screen door Sullivan went, following light at the end of a hallway to the kitchen.

He called, "Sarah! It's Mike," but received no im-mediate answer.

And the kitchen was empty. He looked around—the evening dishes had been put away, the room clean and white. In the kitchen was a large picture window onto the lake, where he could see Michael on the beach, bending to pet the dog.

From a chair in the corner, Harlen Maguire slowly stood. He quickly fired two rounds, hitting Sullivan cleanly. Sullivan staggered and fell, his eyes wide in shock and surprise as he looked at his killer.

Harlen's eyes were unblinking and crazed in a face whose boyish handsomeness had been replaced with a ravaged welter of scars, the aftermath of that shattered crystal lamp in Rance's suite. Maguire put his gun down and got his camera, mounted on a tripod, and into position.

"Smile," the photographer said as he took a picture.

Sullivan struggled, only he was fading. . . . Could he even move his arm . . . ?

Harlen Maguire—who had stowed the body of Sarah McGinnis in a cupboard nearby, just about an hour before—moved in closer, positioning his camera, and began to focus it. He had paid an awful price for this picture—his face would never be right, even with plastic surgery—but this would be the crowning portrait for his gallery of death.

Mike Sullivan—life oozing out of him—would make an excellent subject, a special study in death, since a succession of photos would record the stages of dying . . . one photo would have the glimmer of life in those eyes, the next would show the blankness of death.

The photographer—studying the upside-down image of the slumped, bleeding man—framed his subject carefully . . . no rush. . . .

A tiny noise behind him made Maguire spin toward the doorway . . .

. . . and just behind him stood Sullivan's son—who had taken Maguire's own gun off the kitchen table.

Maguire had been in tight situations before—in the Rance suite, among others—but in those instances he'd been armed. Harlen Maguire suddenly understood that his fascination with death did not extend to experiencing his own.

Michael had known there was trouble when that dog ran up to him on the beach, and the boy had seen blood streaked and caked on the animal's paws.

He'd already been running toward the house when he heard the shots . . .

. . . and now the boy stood pointing the pistol, shaking not with fear for himself but for his father—his wounded father, bleeding on the floor, defenseless, barely awake . . . a fallen soldier. That this could happen to Papa, the boy of course had contemplated; and yet seeing this terrible tableau before him, he wondered how it could be possible. . . . Was this another nightmare?

Whatever it was, he was in it, and his father was in trouble.

For once, Maguire blinked. "Give me the gun."

The gun was shaking in Michael's grasp.

"Michael?" The scarred man had his hands up, and he was smiling a sick sort of smile.

Michael held the gun pointed straight at Harlen.

The man was trying to stay calm. He slowly approached the boy. "Michael, give me the gun."

The boy shifted his gaze to his father, for guidance. *Should I shoot him, Papa?* his eyes asked, but Papa's response, a sort of weave of his head, didn't tell him anything.

"Please . . . kid," the scared scarred man said.

So many feelings pulsed through the boy—rage, determination, fear, desperation—then his finger tightened on the trigger.

A shot rang in the small room—a tiny crack louder than any thunder.

The scarred man looked at Michael, his eyes still dancing wildly; then, like a light had switched off, the eyes were empty, and the man dropped to the floor, a puppet with its strings snipped. A corpse now, the scarred man lay in an awkward, artless sprawl.

Michael, who had not fired, looked over at his fallen father, who had. Smoke spiraled out of the snout of the .45 in Papa's hand, making a question-mark curl.

"I couldn't do it, Papa. . . ." Michael felt ashamed.

But Papa wore the trace of a smile. "I know."

Michael took his father in his arms and held him, held him close but not tight, not wanting to hurt him, cradling Papa's head against his chest, the boy getting blood all over himself, not caring.

The boy looked around them, dead body on the floor, smell of cordite in the air, his father bleeding.

Papa was saying something; Michael had to lean close to hear it: "I'm sorry," his father whispered again and again.

And his father died there, in the boy's arms; yet the boy kept rocking him, for a long time, as if the dead man were a baby he was soothing to sleep.

Outside the window, where the wind whispered through, making ghosts of the sheer curtains, the vast, peaceful expanse of blue that was the lake glistened in the dying sun.

But by the time Michael moved from his late father's side, easing the man to the linoleum floor, the moon was bathing the gently rippling lake in ivory. Michael removed his father's coat, bundled it up into a makeshift pillow, and placed it under Papa's head so he could rest better.

That was the last time I ever held a gun. I understood then that Michael Sullivan's greatest fear was not death, but that his son would follow the same road.

People always thought that I grew up on a farm and I guess in a way I did. But I lived a lifetime before that—in those six weeks on the road with Michael Sullivan in the winter of 1931. When people ask me if he was a decent man, or if there was no good in him at all, I don't answer. I just tell them he was my father.

A Tip of the Fedora

As the author of the original graphic novel, *Road to Perdition* (1998), I am in the unusual position of basing this novel on a screenplay . . . based on my own work.

For those unfamiliar with the term, a "graphic novel" is a book-length work told in comic book style. I feared the original illustrated book would not reach readers who do not regularly partake of the comics medium . . . which is unfortunate, as that medium is as vital and compelling as motion pictures themselves.

I have done my best to honor David Self's fine screenplay, and am particularly grateful to him for heightening the Mike Sullivan/John Rooney father-and-son relationship. The filmmakers have chosen to fictionalize and change the last name of John Looney—the real-life gangster "godfather" of 1920s Rock Island—to "Rooney," and I have honored this change in these pages. Both John and Connor Looney existed, the latter truly nicknamed Crazy

Connor, and a loosely factual basis underlies the tale in my graphic novel.

I stumbled across the story of the Looneys in researching *True Detective* (1983), the first of the Nathan Heller novels, one of three books comprising my *Frank Nitti Trilogy*; the Heller series continues, as does my sporadic series of novels based on the career of Eliot Ness. My research associate on those books, George Hagenauer, offered information and insights during the writing of this work, as well.

The time frame of my original story is consistent with history where Al Capone and Frank Nitti are concerned; however, much of the Looney material is moved up in time from the 1920s (though Looney's organization and the Capone mob were indeed connected). A few other changes have been made; the film's use of the Lone Ranger (I had used Tom Mix exclusively in the graphic novel) had a nice resonance for me, and I retained it—though that character did not make its radio debut until January 1933.

Bj Elsner's *Rock Island: Yesterday, Today and Tomorrow* (1988) was a key reference work for the original graphic novel. The indefatigable Ms. Elsner also provided further background material and came through like a champ for me at a difficult time (our mutual friend, author David Collins, died during the writing of this book).

Thanks also to Bill Wundrum of the *Quad City Times*. Bill got me interested in John Looney in the first place, when I approached him while doing Nathan Heller research; for this novel, I drew upon articles of Bill's as well as several of his locally produced books about the Quad Cities (the Tri-Cities, in John Looney's day). Bill and I met, incidentally, at the Lexington Hotel, the night Geraldo opened Al Capone's vault.

Among many gangland reference works consulted were *Capone* (1971), John Kobler; *Capone* (1994), Lawrence Bergreen; *The Legacy of Al Capone* (1975), George Murray; and *Mr. Capone* (1992), Robert J. Schoenberg. Various WPA Guides on the states through which the Sullivans travel were also used, as was the fine historical picture book, *I Remember Distinctly: A Family Album of the American People in the Years of Peace: 1918 to Pearl Harbor* (1947) by Agnes Rogers and Frederick Lewis Allen. Also, I used the article "Smashing Rock Island's Reign of Terror" by O. F. Claybaugh in the December 1930 issue of *Master Detective*.

I would like to thank my editor Dan Slater of NAL, who provided solid support. Also, the similarly dogged efforts of my friends Dominick Abel and Ken Levin—my literary agent and entertainment lawyer, respectively—were truly above and beyond the call of duty.

Dean Zanuck and his father Richard—producers of the motion picture *Road to Perdition*—also provided invaluable support.

I would also like to acknowledge the illustrator of the original graphic novel, Richard Piers Rayner, who so wonderfully brought this story to life; his artistry had much to do with attracting the attention of Hollywood to this material. Thanks, too, to Andrew Helfer, the graphic novel's editor, whose story sense was unerring; without Andy's dedication to this yarn, and his belief in it, none of this would have happened. Thanks to Paul Levitz of DC Comics for publishing the graphic novel, and helping clear the bramble of rights to enable the writing of this prose version. I urge readers who enjoy this novel—and/or the Sam Mendes film version—to seek out our original work.

I would also like to thank my wife, Barbara Collins, and son, Nathan, for their love, inspiration, and support.

MAX ALLAN COLLINS has earned an unprecedented nine Private Eye Writers of America "Shamus" nominations for his "Nathan Heller" historical thrillers, winning twice (*True Detective*, 1983, and *Stolen Away*, 1991).

A Mystery Writers of America "Edgar" nominee in both fiction and nonfiction categories, Collins has been hailed as "the Renaissance man of mystery fiction." His credits include five suspense-novel series, film criticism, short fiction, songwriting, trading-card sets, and movie tie-in novels, including *In the Line of Fire, Air Force One*, and the *New York Times*–bestselling *Saving Private Ryan*.

He scripted the internationally syndicated comic strip DICK TRACY from 1977 to 1993, is cocreator of the comic-book features MS. TREE, WILD DOG, and MIKE DANGER, and has written the BATMAN comic book and newspaper strip. His graphic novel *Road to Perdition* is the basis of the DreamWorks feature film starring Tom Hanks and Paul Newman, directed by Sam Mendes.

Working as an independent filmmaker in his native Iowa, he wrote and directed the acclaimed suspense film *Mommy*, starring Patty McCormack, premiering on Lifetime in 1996; Collins performed the same duties for a well-received 1997 sequel, *Mommy's Day*. He also wrote *The Expert*, a 1995 HBO World Premiere film, and wrote and directed an award-winning documentary, *Mike Hammer's Mickey Spillane* (1999). His third independent feature, the innovative *Real Time: Siege at Lucas Street Market* (2001), is a DVD from Troma.

Collins lives in Muscatine, Iowa, with his wife, writer Barbara Collins, and their teenage son, Nathan.